GILLIAM COUNTY LIBRARY
P9-DVF-704

This book donated by

The Libri Foundation
Eugene, Oregon

AWAY RUNNING

AWAY RUNNING

DAVID WRIGHT AND LUC BOUCHARD

ORCA BOOK PUBLISHERS

Library and Archives Canada Cataloguing in Publication

Bouchard, Luc, 1963 June 6-, author
Away running / Luc Bouchard and David Wright. —
Junior Library Guild edition.

Issued in print and electronic formats.
ISBN 978-1-4598-1379-3 (bound)—ISBN 978-1-4598-1046-4 (paperback).—
ISBN 978-1-4598-1047-1 (pdf).— ISBN 978-1-4598-1048-8 (epub)

I. Wright, David, 1964–, author II. Title.
PS8603.O92435A93 2016 jc813'.6 C2015-908794-5

First published in the United States, 2016
Library of Congress Control Number: 2015946245

Summary: In this novel for teens, Matt and Free meet in Paris, where they both play American football on a team in a poverty-stricken suburb where racial tension affects the team.

Orca Book Publishers is dedicated to preserving the environment and has printed this book on Forest Stewardship Council® certified paper.

Orca Book Publishers gratefully acknowledges the support for its publishing programs provided by the following agencies: the Government of Canada through the Canada Book Fund and the Canada Council for the Arts, and the Province of British Columbia through the BC Arts Council and the Book Publishing Tax Credit.

Cover design by Teresa Bubela
Cover images by Getty Images and Dreamstime.com
Author photos by Jonathan Wei, Julie Durocher

ORCA BOOK PUBLISHERS
www.orcabook.com

Printed and bound in Canada.

19 18 17 16 • 4 3 2 1

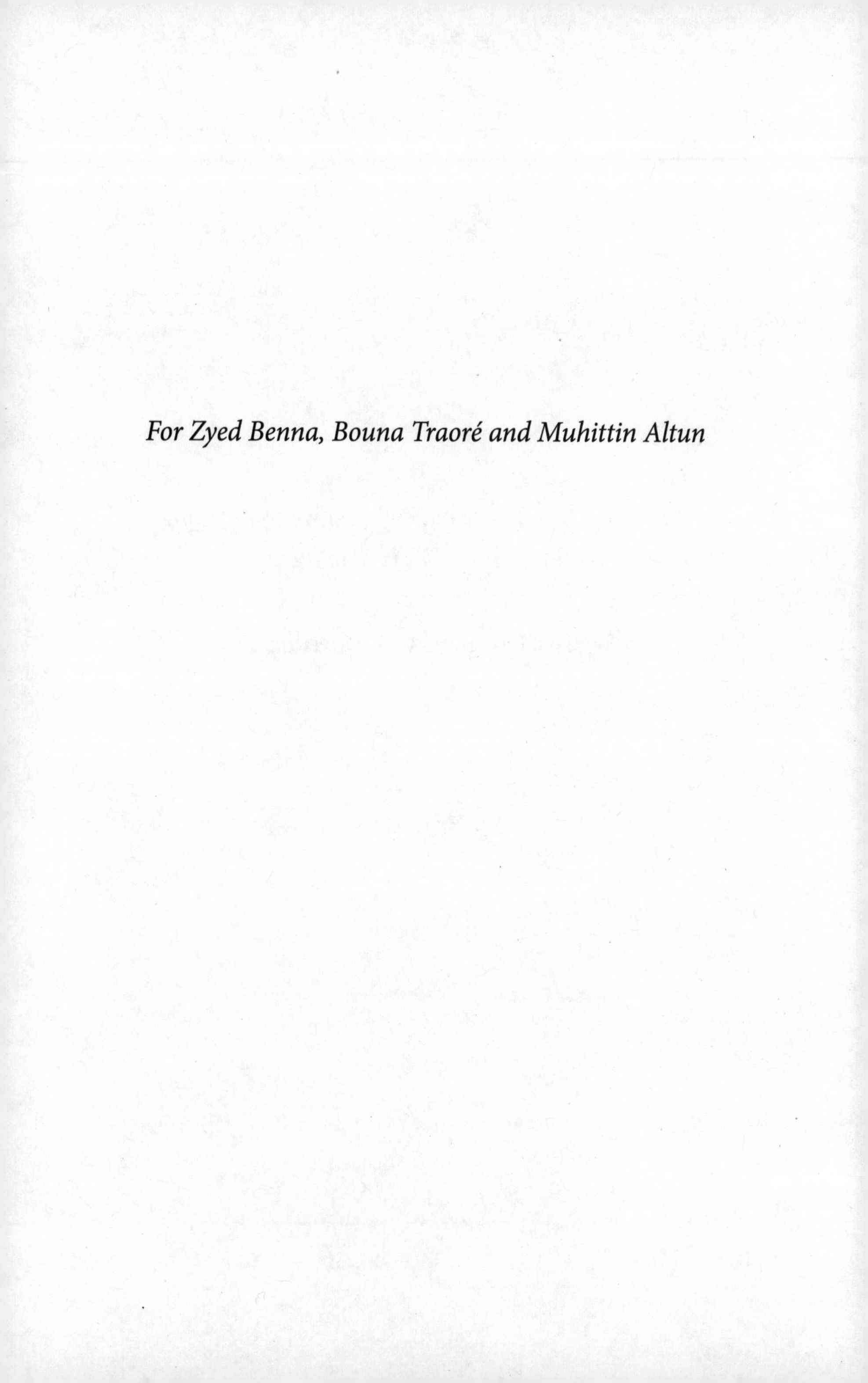

For Zyed Benna, Bouna Traoré and Muhittin Altun

But Paris was a very old city and we were young and nothing was simple there.

—Ernest Hemingway, *A Moveable Feast*

VILLENEUVE-LA-GRANDE
APRIL 15

The Wednesday before game day—our last game of the season, for the league championship—me and Matt take the suburban train, the RER, from Paris up to Villeneuve-La-Grande early, way before practice. Me and him play American football for the team there, the Diables Rouges. We meet a bunch of our teammates outside the station and walk to a field between some abandoned cinder-block warehouses and their high school to play a pickup game of soccer.

A few guys from their projects join us, including Karim and one of his crew. Me and Karim got history, dating back to when I first got here, in February. Him and his set were slinging dime bags outside their high-rise like the bangers do back in my 'hood in San Antonio, and he just strode up on me, spitting French slang I didn't understand at the time, but I squared off with him all the same. That's what you do when someone's fronting on you.

Now he acts like he doesn't remember or doesn't care. But Matt whispers in English, "Keep cool, Freeman. We'll be going home soon. No more Karim."

I'm like, "Tsst. I ain't studying that fool."

Never having to see Karim again is the last thing I think on when I think of home. I think about Mama, my brother Tookie and baby sister Tina, who I haven't seen in so long—you know I do. But I also think about not seeing Matt anymore, him going back to Montreal and off to college to major in business and become a big businessman like almost everyone else in his family. I'm going to miss every single one of the Diables Rouges. Even Moose. We've gotten pretty close since our rough start. That's what I think on when I think about leaving.

Moose takes charge now. "The two '*Ricains*," he says, pointing to me and Matt, "with me, Jean-Marc and Couly. Sidi, you and Mobylette take Adar, Franck, Karim and...?"

He's looking at Karim's boy.

"Omar," Karim's boy says, doing that dope-smoker giggle thing as he pulls his hoodie off over his head.

Like so many here, the field is more dirt than grass and the goals don't have nets, but there's a brick wall surrounding the lot, so we shouldn't have to go chasing after too many missed kicks. Adar pulls a ball out of his book bag and kicks the game off.

Matt insists on covering Karim—or trying to. Karim is cat quick. He plays with a cigarette dangling from his lips (that pisses Matt off even more) and dribbles circles around Matt.

I'm no better. I play cornerback and am fit, but all you do in soccer is run, and every few seconds I'm bent over at the waist and wheezing. (I think Moose put me and Matt on the same side to humiliate us *'Ricains*, as the guys call us North Americans, even more.)

And I notice something: *everybody* is loose today—all our teammates. Sidi pulls Moose's T-shirt over his head to steal his dribble. Jean-Marc and Mobylette and Adar play grab-ass as much as soccer. They don't act nothing like before, like after we beat the Anges Bleus and then the Caïmans and everybody pretended like it was no big deal but they were all sniping at each other and practices were a disaster. This week, the week of the last game of our season, everybody is Zen.

Karim passes the ball to Sidi, and I cover him. Sidi plays it serious, dribbling forward, shifting his weight to keep his body between me and the ball. Nearing the box, he does this dope scissors move where he switches it from one foot to the other, and then he fires it into the goal.

Dang!

I jog back upfield. "I'll never again in my life look down on the sport of soccer," I say, saying *soccer* in English, the rest *en français*.

"Football," Moose corrects me, pronouncing it in French—FOO-tuh-bowl. "*This* is the real football, not what we do with the Diables Rouges." He jogs ahead, teasing, "All the world calls it by its proper name but you bullheaded '*Ricains*."

The sun is setting. Matt points to the incoming black clouds. "It's going to rain a river."

"Should be a great practice tonight then," I say. "Slogging around and drenched and no footing."

"I hope the weather clears by Sunday," Matt adds, looking worried.

Matt is our starting QB, but it's not about stats with him. Rain will make a mess of our passing game, and everybody knows, our opponents included, that we need the pass if we're going to win on Sunday. A heavy, slick ball will make Matt's job all the harder.

We play a little while longer, till it gets too dark to continue, then call it quits. We have to grab our gear from the clubhouse and then get to practice on time, and we're cutting it a little close. Still, everybody is laughing, boasting about his best play (except me and Matt—there's not much to boast about).

Moose grabs Karim from behind in a bear hug and lifts him off his feet. "How many times do I have to say it, *mec*? You've got crazy quicks. We could use you on the Diables Rouges."

Mec means "guy," but up here they use it kind of like we do back home, like *dawg* or *G* or whatnot.

Karim flips the hood of his sweatshirt up over his head, strikes a match and puts it to his cigarette, the glow lighting up his face. "Naw. Sports is your thing. I've got other interests."

"The Diables treat us right, Karim, no joke," Moose says. "City hall finds guys work, stuff like that."

"City jobs." He pulls hard on his smoke, the tip burning bright. "My pay scale is higher."

Karim's friend Omar laughs, and he and Karim head off in the other direction from us.

"*Oueche!*" Karim calls over his shoulder. Yo! "Kill those bourgeois pricks Sunday."

The rest of us, ten or twelve or so, walk down the street, past an abandoned warehouse, its windows all busted out, a machine shop and a funeral home, then along the corrugated tin fence of a darkened construction site.

Sidi says, "I know a shortcut."

"Through the site?" Moose sounds reluctant.

"It'll save us fifteen minutes."

Sidi climbs up onto the padlocked chain-link gate and jumps down on the other side. Matt follows suit, and I follow him.

Moose stays outside. "My father" is all he says.

And I'm thinking, He's right, duh! Moose's dad keeps a pretty tight rein on him. I'm about to climb back over when Sidi says, "C'mon, you wimp," and Mobylette and the others climb over too.

Moose doesn't move.

It's pitch-black inside the site, all of us just shadows against more shadows. The Cité des Cinq Mille, the high-rise projects where most of the guys live, looms ahead of us, pushing up past the far-side fence, two football fields away. Most of its windows are lit up.

Finally, Moose says, "But nobody screws around in there." He points his finger through the chain-link directly at Sidi's dark shape. "Nobody! Understood?"

"Okay, okay already," Sidi says.

Then Moose hops the fence.

Once my eyes adjust, I see that there are stacks of two-by-fours and two-by-sixes and rebar all over. A yellow-and-black hydraulic excavator stands there like a sleeping Decepticon, its giant metal arm and bucket still. I kind of want to warn the others to tiptoe by, so we don't wake it. Then Sidi jumps up onto the tracks of the digging machine, opens his arms wide and in thick-accented English yells, "I'm the King of the Woooorrrld!"

We all laugh. Even Moose.

"Come on," he tells Sidi. "Get down."

We work our way through the rows of stacked gear and metal pipes. At the gate on the other side, we climb up and jump over. Just as the last one of us drops to the ground, the night is suddenly blue-lit, and there's a siren. Then another. Two white cars, engines roaring, *POLICE* in block letters across each hood, bear down on us. A third rounds the corner. I think I can hear a fourth.

We all freeze.

"I don't have my ID papers," Sidi says.

"Me neither," says Mobylette.

"*Merde*," says Moose.

The first two cars scream forward, sirens blaring.

"We didn't do anything," Matt says. "We'll be okay."

But they ignore him.

"That means they'll take us in," Sidi says. "Call our parents."

"*Merde!*" says Moose again.

He looks freaked. Panicked.

The cars screech to a stop not ten feet from us, one blocking us to the right, the other to the left. Six cops in civilian clothes spring out, carrying those huge

Flash-Ball guns. They grab Adar and Ibrahim, tossing them to the ground.

The cops are screaming, "*Par terre, par terre!*"—On the ground!—and "*Tout de suite! Allez, bougez-vous!*"—Right now! Go, move!

Me and Matt, we raise our hands, but Moose and Sidi and Mobylette, they break. So fast the cops don't immediately react. They just kind of follow with their eyes, looking unsure what to do. I watch Moose and them running too, as surprised as the cops are.

"Don't move, or we fire!" one says, pointing his Flash-Ball directly at my chest.

"*Halte!*" another screams after Moose and Sidi and Mobylette.

Two cops take off after them on foot. One of the cars peels off, its siren blowing, shrill and insistent.

A cop throws me to the ground, driving his shoe into the back of my neck.

"Easy, podner," I say in English.

"*Arrêtes de bouger*," he says—Stop moving.

"You're crushing my neck!"

"*Ta gueule!*" the cop screams—Shut your trap.

Matt is on the ground now too.

The bottom chassis of the police car, the axle and tires, frames my view. An officer frisks me, empties my pockets, then handcuffs me. I can hear dogs barking off in the distance.

"*Debout!*" the cops are all screaming at us. Get up! Now!

It ain't as easy as it sounds, lying on our bellies like that, hands cuffed behind our backs. Matt says so, and the officer he says it to grabs his cuffed hands and wrenches him to his feet.

Matt's scream sends a chill down my spine.

They line the nine of us up against a police van that has arrived. There are three more cars now too, blue lights flashing. We didn't do anything wrong, but still I feel kind of guilty, standing there in the glare of their lights. I glance at Matt. He's sweaty, all dirty from the ground.

"We know you broke into the construction site to steal," one of the cops says calmly.

None of us says anything. The cops don't either, not for a long time. They just stand there staring at us, their Flash-Balls still out.

"What did you vandalize?" one cop says finally. "If we have to go in and figure it out ourselves, it's going to be much worse for you."

Another long silence.

"Some of you don't have papers. How can we know you even have the right to be in France?"

A cop off to the side scrutinizes me and Matt, our passports in his hand, then walks over to the cop in charge, the one who has been speaking. He points from our passports to us. The head cop indicates for him to pull us out of the line. The cop grabs each of us by an arm and pushes us ahead of him toward the top guy, who says, "You shouldn't be running around with a bunch of hoodlums."

The cop who separated me and Matt from the rest stares at us—hard—while the other flips through our passports. Then it occurs to me: Can they deport us for this? Will we have to miss our last game? And what'll Mama say?

The cops start shepherding the other guys into the back of the police van. Some have their ID cards, some don't—it doesn't matter.

"Check my papers," Adar is saying. "They're fine."

"We didn't do anything," says Jean-Marc. "We were just taking a shortcut to practice."

"*Vos gueules*!" the head cop says—Shut up! "You broke into a locked construction site to vandalize and steal. You're going to jail."

A cop comes toward me and Matt, but the head guy waves him off and then goes to one of the cars, where he sits behind the wheel, one foot out on the ground, leaving me and Matt standing there while the other cops push our friends—our teammates!—into the back of the van.

"Should be us going in too, right alongside them," I say as the van pulls off.

Matt says, "You're right, Free, but I can't help it—I feel kind of relieved." He looks me in my eye, then quickly looks down at his feet.

I look away too.

The head cop talks into the radio in the car, one foot jackhammering up and down as he stares over at us. He looks disappointed, like he knows us and entrusted us with some simple task—feeding the dog or taking out the trash—and we didn't do it.

The cop who pulled us out of the line joins him in the car, the only car left. I hear the radio, staticky and distant but clear: "...three fugitives are in flight at the cemetery. Four officers in pursuit..."

"That's Moose and Sidi and Mobylette," I whisper to Matt.

Matt stays stiff, steady, staring at his feet. "We weren't doing anything!" he suddenly yells toward the car. "We were just trying to get to practice on time!"

The head cop gets out and storms over. "*Arrêtes ton cinéma*. You think this is a game?"

"We were just crossing the site. We didn't do anything."

"And you think that's what this is about?" he tells Matt. "Take a look around you, *mon petit gars*. This isn't Canada. This is France's gutter. Half the population lives off drug dealing and petty theft. And the hatred, the anti-police and anti-white hatred..."

He stops, but not because of me, because I'm black and he's just showed his ass. It's as though he sees me like Matt, as white. The cop stands there staring straight at us.

Matt doesn't drop his eyes. "We play for the American football team," he says, calm now, like he can reason with the guy. "All of us do. The municipality sponsors the team."

"And?" the head cop says. "You think that means something?"

The radio crackles: "...heading toward the electrical substation. We need backup..."

The cop heads to the car. "If those boys aren't in the system," he says, "well, then, they have nothing to worry about. They'll be back in their beds later tonight."

He makes a gesture to the other officer, who comes over.

"My boss seems to think you're okay," the cop says, unlocking Matt first. "Me, I know better. Americans or not, you boys were into something." He looks me, then Matt, in the eye. "But he thinks we should let you go, and it's his call." He walks back toward the police car. "Get out of here. This is no place for tourists."

He gets in, and the car pulls away.

"Dang," I say, rubbing my wrists where the handcuffs dug in.

Matt kneads his shoulder.

"Dang," I say again. "What do we do now?"

We just stand there in the empty lot beside the construction site.

"I don't know, Free," he says. "Go to practice?"

"What about Moose and Sidi and Mobylette?"

We stand there.

"Let's go to Moose's building," I say.

"And do what? We can't tell his father!"

"Of course not," I say, "but if Moose gets away, that's where he'll head. Or to the clubhouse."

"And if he and Sidi and Mobylette don't get away?" He's still kneading his shoulder.

"If they don't get away?" I say. "Dang."

THREE MONTHS EARLIER
JANUARY 10

MATHIEU "MATT" DUMAS

I remember the day I decided to come to Paris. Decided? I'm not sure that's the right word for it, exactly. It started on a January afternoon like any other. I'd popped over to my school to see if class lists had been posted for the coming semester (my last!), hoping I'd run into friends (I didn't). I was walking down Sainte-Catherine toward my mom's condo. It was snowy and cold, the wind cutting—a typical Montreal winter.

Jean-Michel opened the door as I approached. "Congratu-freakin-lations!" he said. He wore a full-length dark wool coat against the cold, and one of those funny hats doormen always wear. "I saw your name in *Le Journal de Montréal*. Laval University, huh?"

I knew an article was coming out, announcing the university's football recruits, but I didn't know it would be that day.

My dad always said it was unseemly to boast. *Act like you've been there before*, he'd say. So I said, "Yep," trying to keep cool, but I found it impossible not to smile. "I'll be joining the number-one team in the country."

"I'm a McGill fan myself," Jean-Michel said, stepping into the lobby behind me. "And hockey more than football, frankly."

"No way! Hockey is just body checks and brawling. Football is ballet by comparison."

He pushed the call button for the lift and handed me our mail. The doors slid open, I walked into the glass elevator and entered our five-digit code, and the doors slid shut. My dad would tell me I was lucky to be living at the Crystal Towers, but I found the place so tacky, everything gilded and gaudy and shiny new, that I was embarrassed to invite friends over. My mom had moved us there after she and my dad split up, pretending she'd chosen it with me in mind, to be closer to my school. Right.

The lift shot up the outside wall of the building. Snow wafted down over the already white city. The giant Christmas tree across the street beside Air France's Canadian headquarters was still up. Two blocks away,

I could see the Bell Centre, home of the Montreal Canadiens.

I was looking forward to seeing the newspaper article, but I felt uneasy too. I mean, would I even see any playing time at Laval? The coach had told me they were bringing in three other quarterbacks, and I knew that one, this kid from Plattsburgh, New York, was supposed to be a stud. I'd googled him. The article called him "Laval's #1 prospect," and his stats were studly, that was for sure.

The elevator opened onto our penthouse, and I headed toward the kitchen, where I dropped the mail onto the quartz countertop. The newspaper wasn't there, but the answering machine blinked red. "You. Have. Three. New. Messages," the android voice said.

The first was from that morning, from Jean-Michel. "Matt, we've received a special delivery for you. From France." It was the large beige envelope I'd just dropped onto the counter. It felt like a magazine, and by the return address—*Club Villeneuvien de Football Américain*—I recognized that it was from Moose, whom I'd met the summer before.

The second message was from my girlfriend, Céline. "What's going on? I've been trying to reach you on your cell all day. You ignoring my calls? Caaaall me." Later, I thought. I just didn't have the energy for her right then.

The third message was the one that got to me. It was for my mom, but it was from the dean of Orford University, and it was about me. "*Bonjour*, Madame Tremblay," the machine said. "This is Pierre Cartier. I wanted to let you know I've followed up personally on your son's case. Mathieu should receive the official letter in the next few days; I've posted it Express Mail. I'll see you at our next board meeting."

I replayed the message twice before it sank in. My mom had been pulling strings again in her push for me to attend Orford. And my mom got what she wanted. She'd wanted to be a journalist, and she became the editor of one of Canada's most popular women's magazines. She'd wanted to leave my dad, and here we were in our tacky penthouse. Now Mom wanted me to go to Orford, which had no football team, not even a bad one, but was the top business program in the country; she wanted me to major in business administration like my brother Marc and sister Manon had, and to get an MBA or a law degree after.

Marc is a corporate lawyer who works in Shanghai for China National Petroleum. Manon makes tons of dough as a stockbroker in Toronto. Making money, that's what *they* wanted. Me, I wanted to play football.

"You're home early," Claude said, scaring the hell out of me.

"Don't sneak up on me," I told him.

His laugh was more like a cackle. "Just passing through," he said, heading toward the elevator. He had the folded newspaper under his arm. "Your mother asked me to pick up the invitations for the fundraiser tonight. She also told me to tell you there's lasagna in the fridge."

I didn't know if my mom had met Claude before or after the divorce, but I did know he was spending more and more time at the penthouse. Fine, just as long as he quit acting all buddy-buddy with me. And as long as he didn't try to play dad.

He waved goodnight and got in the lift. I flipped through the rest of the mail, thinking, There'd better not be anything addressed to Claude…

I had one more letter, this one from the Northern Bank of Canada. I took it and the manila envelope from Moose to my room and sat on my bed. (A king, of course. It was so huge I'd had to leave my NFL-team-helmet sheets at the old house, with Dad.)

Moose (his real name is Moussa Oussekine) had sent the most recent issue of *US Football Magazine*, a French version of *Sports Illustrated* that reported exclusively on American-style football. On the cover was a great shot of the Diables Rouges quarterback. The QB stood tall in the pocket, arm cocked, ready to dart a pass, as defenders in black and gold swarmed around. The Diables unis looked like vintage Arizona Cardinals gear but with a trident on the helmets instead of the bird. There was a huge crowd in the stands.

Moose was the captain of the Junior Diables Rouges, the Under-20s side. I'd met him during two-a-days the summer before, when he came with a group of other French players to take part in my team's preseason training camp. The French guys stayed with host families. My dad is our head coach, and Moose stayed at my old house with him the entire two weeks. I'd go over after practices, and Moose and I would watch game film in my dad's office and play *Madden NFL* for hours.

Flipping through the pages of the magazine, I stumbled on a Post-it note on the opening page of the Under-20s season preview. Moose had scribbled: *Oueche, Matt! Yo, the season kicks off in a few weeks. You need to get your ass to France and throw some long bombs for us.*

I laughed. Moose had been harping at me about going there to play for the Diables since the day I met him, but, of course, I'd never taken it seriously.

The French played their season in the winter and spring. The article described the twenty-five Under-20s teams across the country, focusing mostly on the seven in the Premier Division. Of those seven, *US Football* ranked the Diables Rouges sixth. They'd finish first with me as quarterback, I thought. Not boasting, just saying.

I put the magazine down and turned on the flat-screen TV on the wall across from my bed. Along with the giant bed, my mom had bought me the TV and a new iMac. Like *that* would make this place home. I zapped from channel to channel while the snow fell steadily outside my window. Nasty weather, all slush and cold.

I booted up the iMac and checked my emails. I had two new ones. The first was a mass-mail about women's rights in Afghanistan from my cousin Juliette, who was doing her doctorate at the Sorbonne in Paris. The other was from my dad. Going ice fishing for a few days, he'd written in French. No cell reception. Call the village store if something comes up. They'll know where to find me.

Since my parents split up, every chance he got he headed up to the cottage he inherited from my grandfather, to bow-hunt or fly-fish or chop wood or whatever. He just needed the time alone in the wilderness. And I understood why: I needed my own wilderness too—what with the Orford/Laval thing, with my mom and all her expectations.

I'd forgotten about the second envelope, from Northern Bank of Canada. It looked real official. At the top of the letter, it said *RE: Mathieu Dumas RÉGIMES D'ÉPARGNE-ÉTUDES.* My "Education Savings Plan"? I skimmed all the banky kind of stuff but stopped when I got to the last line: *Fonds disponibles* (funds available): $84,900.

Eighty-four thousand dollars!

I went back over the letter more slowly, looking for the catch. I knew my mom had a notecard in her desk drawer with our bank information on it. I got it, googled the bank's website and entered the client-card number, user name and password. It took a few seconds to get to my personal page, but there it was: Education Savings Plan.

I didn't even know I had one.

I clicked and a new window opened, identical to the letter I was holding in my hand. Yep, $84,900.

I looked at the magazine beside me on the bed, at the Diables Rouges QB in his flashy red uni, the trident on the helmet and the roaring crowd. I didn't usually talk to myself—I mean, who does?—but I heard myself saying aloud, "Seriously, Matt? Are you going to do this?"

I clicked on the link to transfer or withdraw funds.

It asked me to enter the amount. I typed my two favorite jersey numbers, 88 and 15.

A window popped up that said the maximum daily withdrawal amount was $2,000.

I typed 2,000 instead.

The pop-up showed a tiny clock, the second hand ticking. Then, *Confirmer la transaction?*

I swiveled my desk chair left and right, left and right.

"Matt, seriously?"

Left and right, left and right.

I clicked on the link to confirm the withdrawal.

Fifteen minutes later, Jean-Michel held the door open for me as I headed outside. "You look like a man on a mission," he said.

I didn't answer. I was carrying my backpack, and I crossed the boulevard, heading for the Air France building. Northern Bank had a branch there, beside the airline office. The snow kept falling, and my footsteps erased themselves behind me.

MATT

And that's how I ended up in Paris seventeen hours later. The woman at the information desk at Charles de Gaulle airport gave me a map, and I found my cousin Juliette's street. I rode the RER train to her stop, Cité Universitaire. My first impressions, rising up into the city on the escalator: the air was brisk, but the sun was out and bright; there was a bustling boulevard, and Renaults and Peugeots and Mercedes sped by, honking; a green-and-white accordion bus stopped to pick up passengers. Just to my right was a park, the Parc Montsouris.

Paris was hillier than I remembered from the time my family had come here when Marc and Manon still lived at home and I was just a little kid. On the other side of the park were gray stone six-floor walk-ups, and three blocks past that, in a narrow alleyway, was Juliette's building. It was probably as old as Canada, and its entrance was a massive porte cochere. I pushed open the huge oak doors and stumbled into a little old lady hunched over a green plastic broom.

"*Bonjour, Madame*," I greeted her.

"*Jeune homme*"—Young man—she replied, all but ignoring me.

An interior cobblestone courtyard led to a stairway in the back. All the apartments had tall windows, leafy plants dangling in nearly every one, even at this time of year. The wooden stairs creaked as I climbed. The second floor is called the first here, the second is the third and so on. When I got seven floors up, I stopped, kind of winded, before knocking at 6G.

Juliette's jaw dropped when she saw me. Literally. She stood there, her mouth hanging open. "Matt? What are you doing here?" she said finally.

"You invited me, remember?"

"Sure, but I imagined you'd call first."

We hugged, and she waved me in. Her apartment was tiny. Two steps in, and I was in the middle of the living room.

"Did I catch you at a bad time?" I asked.

"Well, actually, I have to leave in a minute. I have a couple of seminars."

"Want me to come back later?"

"Of course not, silly."

She bounced around the room, from the desk in the corner through an adjoining door and then back to the couch, where there were stacks of books and papers. She put a few things in her satchel and then straightened up. Pointing to the couch, she indicated a space she'd just cleared for me.

"How long you in town for?"

"Depends," I told her, but I figured it wasn't the best time to try to explain. "But go on to your seminars. We can talk when you get back."

She grabbed her keys and purse but came to a stop to ask, "How is Lucie? Charles?"

By her tone of voice when she said *Charles*, it was clear she was more interested in my dad, her mother's brother. Everybody knew he was the one who was having the harder time with the divorce.

"They're fine," I told her. "Both of them."

"Look, I really have to go. Make yourself at home. If you go out..." She pointed to a set of keys hanging from a nail on the wall.

I got up from the couch and gave her a huge hug.

"I'm really glad to see you, Matt." There were actually tears in her eyes. "We'll catch up properly when I get back at dinnertime—seven or eight."

She left, and suddenly it hit me: I was in Paris! I was standing in an apartment the size of my bedroom back home. The sagging wooden beams that ran the length of the ceiling looked like something out of *Les Misérables*; there was a half-eaten baguette on the table and a bowl with drops of café au lait still in the bottom. I was in Paris!

The apartment had a kitchenette and a tiny bedroom with space for a futon and a dresser. The bathroom was just a commode and a sink, four feet by four feet, a hand-held shower against one wall. The shower was great though—a strong stream, and hot! After the long, sleepless night on the plane, I stripped and enjoyed it—for, like, maybe three minutes, until the tiny water heater on the shelf above my head kicked on, and the spray went from scalding to lukewarm to cold.

Okay, I thought. I'll get used to that.

The plan I'd devised on the flight over was to stay with Juliette until I got hold of Moose and looked into joining the Diables Rouges. I didn't know how it worked or even if they had a spot for me on the roster. But this would be *my* cottage in the wilderness. I didn't need the credits at school to graduate, and while I was here, I could figure out the rest.

All the tightness of the previous seventeen hours released as I lay down on Juliette's futon. But even though I hadn't slept one second of the flight over,

I wasn't sleepy at all. Juliette had tacked pictures on her wall—her parents (my uncle Max and aunt Christie) and her sister, Jeanne. There was even one of her and me.

We went back a long way. She used to babysit me from when I was, like, seven until I was twelve. And I'd never forget the last time she did. It was a warm summer night, and my parents were out at the movies or something. I woke up, startled and sweaty, and headed to the kitchen for a glass of water. The lights were out, and there was a rustling kind of noise in the front room. I was about to ask what was going on when I *saw* what was going on: Juliette was naked and squatting like a frog on her boyfriend's lap, her bum *clap-clap-clapping* against his hairy thighs.

I'll carry a Polaroid of Juliette's pasty derriere in my mind for the rest of my days. I mean, I'd seen stuff like that before on the Net—who hasn't?—but it was way better in 3-D. I got down on all fours and hid behind the door to get a better view. And that's when her boyfriend saw me.

Juliette chased me into my room and smacked me. "You say one thing about this to your mom, and I'll tell her about the time I caught you whacking off while you spied on me in the shower."

"But I never did that!"

"Says who?"

She'd slammed the door as she left.

So maybe Juliette and me being roommates wasn't a gimme like I'd hoped. I figured I'd better start making a plan B for lodging just in case.

I switched on my phone. The second it found a network, it started to vibrate and ping. There were at least twenty voice mails and text messages, either Mom or Dad or Céline in the display screen. I didn't open any of them. I punched out a message to Moose instead, in French: **Am in Paris.** I hit *Send.*

He replied almost instantly. **Rite, n Im @ Hogwarts. Landed this a.m.**

My phone rang less than a minute later. "*No way!*" Moose said. "You could have told me you were coming. How long you here for? When do I get to see you?"

"Right now if you want."

"I'm in school, *mec*."

There was a pause.

"Look, I made an excuse of needing to go to the bathroom. I've got to get back to class, but I can bail at lunch. Where's your hotel?"

"Not a hotel. My cousin's place." I gave him the address.

"I'll come get you. We'll head up here and you can check out the team, meet my teammates."

"You guys still looking for a QB?"

"Seriously?"

"Yeah, seriously."

"*Putain, mec!* You're just full of surprises." There was another pause. "Listen, it'll be like, two forty-five or three before I can get down there."

"Great," I said, and we hung up. And before I even felt it coming on, I was out cold.

The sound of arguing in the courtyard filtered up to the window, waking me. The clock on the nightstand read four thirty. *Crap!* There were five new voice mails from home and a long list of texts; I'd managed to sleep through the pinging. One of the texts was from Juliette, saying my mom had called. It ended with **We need to talk.**

Double crap flashed across my mind, even though it was inevitable that Mom would figure it out. My backpack was gone from the closet, my passport from the desk…

Another text was from Moose, just minutes before Juliette's: **Am at your building. Concierge threatening to call cops. WHERE ARE YOU!?!**

Crap, crap, crap!

I hit him back: **Be right down.**

I threw on my clothes and rushed downstairs. The concierge stood beneath the porte cochere, broom in hand, blocking the entrance to the building. Moose and another guy were outside on the street. They wore baggy jeans and red Diables Rouges hoodies, and I could tell that the commotion that had woken me up had come from Moose. Tall and lean, with olive skin and curly dark hair, he was in the little old lady's face, talking excitedly; the other guy, who looked to be in his twenties, was holding Moose back, trying to calm him.

"They're with me," I explained to the concierge. "They're friends."

"No trespassers are allowed in the building," she snapped.

The sharpness of her anger surprised me. "Then why did you let me in this morning?"

She glared at me, holding her broom the way a hockey player holds his stick in a face-off.

"What's going on?" Juliette said, coming in from the street.

The concierge pointed to Moose and his friend with the end of her broom. "These two, they tried to force their way into the building."

"We did no such thing!" said Moose. "We're here to pick up Matt!"

"This is a secure building," she shouted back. "Visitors must be announced!"

"All visitors," Moose said, "or just the North African ones?"

"All right, enough!" Juliette said. She turned to the old lady. "These are guests of my cousin, Madame Lafarge."

"You know full well that all visitors must be announced. This one"—she pointed her broom at me—"as well as those."

"I know, and I will in the future."

"Be sure you do." The old lady stood there for a long moment before finally turning and heading back to her booth.

I ushered us all out into the street. Juliette ignored Moose and his friend and shot me a look—not a friendly one. "I talked to your mother," she said.

"Yeah?"

"Don't play dumb."

"Look, Jules, I wanted to explain this morning, but there was no time—you had to run out. Now I have to go with Moose and meet my—"

"Your mother is furious with me. She's accusing me of encouraging you to come here and a bunch of other things I did not do. I left my seminar early. You owe me an explanation."

"And I'll give you one." Moose and his friend were at their car, a little white Peugeot hatchback, and I moved toward them. "Just not now. I have to go now."

"Mathieu!"

"Trust me, Juliette," I said, one foot in the car. "Please."

Her face was flushed. I could see tears pooling in her eyes, different from the ones she'd greeted me with earlier. Then she turned and entered her building.

MATT

The entire car vibrated as Moose's friend sped over the cobblestone streets of Juliette's neighborhood. The tiny Peugeot only had front seats; I was on the passenger side, and Moose was in the cargo space behind, sitting yoga-style, hunched over and head hanging, his friend scolding him. "Your father taught you better than this. And toward a woman, no less!"

But I was hardly listening. I sat there with my heart racing, my stomach churning, remembering the look on Juliette's face and fretting about whether Moose's invitation had been serious or not. Because I needed it to be. I needed his team to take me on, I needed for them to find me a place to stay. I needed this to be real or else I was on the next flight back to Montreal, my tail between my legs...

Moose's friend pulled the car onto a sort of highway called the Périphérique, the ring road that circled the city. Scooters and motorcycles zipped by on all sides, weaving between speeding cars and giant eighteen-wheelers, everyone honking. Moose's friend was still dogging Moose, and when I looked back, Moose's eyes were glassy.

And I'll be honest, I felt like I was about to cry too. "Look," I said, but neither of them seemed to notice.

"Look," I said again, only louder, and Moose's friend settled down. "I'm sorry to have gotten you guys into that mess. I didn't know. I mean, I just didn't know."

I felt Moose's hand on my shoulder. "No worries, *mec*. It's okay."

We rode in silence, surrounded by revving engines and honking horns. After a while Moose said, "I haven't even introduced you yet. Matt, this is Yazid, a *grand frère*."

A big brother? I thought Moose had told me he was the oldest in his family. But that would explain the reaming out the guy had given Moose.

Yazid freed a hand from the wheel for me to shake; in the crazy Paris traffic, I kind of wished he hadn't.

"I work security for the city of Villeneuve-La-Grande." His smile was really warm. "I also coach the Diables Rouges bantam flag team. If all goes well when you meet Marc Lebrun, maybe you'll give me a hand with them."

Apparently I hadn't completely blown it. Well, at least not with the Diables Rouges.

Yet.

"Marc Lebrun?" I asked.

"He's our club president," Moose said. "I called to tell him you were in town and interested in joining the team."

Meeting the club president?

This was going to be like a job interview. I'd only ever had one job—the summer before, I'd worked for my high school's grounds crew because my dad said that living with Mom was making me soft and too careless about money. There was no interview because my dad is the head coach. I just showed up.

Moose must have sensed my nervousness. "Marc's really great," he said, and he clapped me on the back. "Don't sweat it. He's looking forward to meeting you."

Yazid pulled off the highway into an industrial zone: giant cinder-block buildings that looked to be abandoned factories; in the distance, high-rise projects. It was my introduction to Villeneuve, and I thought it looked like a sci-fi set, desolate and gray.

"I didn't know you had a big brother," I said to Moose, "much less one who plays and coaches for the team."

"A big brother?"

Both Moose and Yazid laughed.

"I introduced Yazid as a *grand frère*, but he's not *my* big brother."

Yazid explained. "We *grands frères*, me and other guys from the neighborhood, watch out for the younger ones. You know, with all the drugs and gangs, the violence." He looked pointedly in the rearview at Moose. "We try to steer them away from trouble."

"Leave it alone, Yaz," Moose said.

"Why should I?" Yazid said. "You afraid of what your friend's going to think?"

I glanced back at Moose, hunched over in the too-tight cargo hold. *Moose and drugs and gangs? Really?*

I realized I didn't really know Moose. We had gotten close real fast in Montreal. I'd introduced him to Céline and most of my friends, and we'd kept texting after he went back to France. But sitting in this car with him and a big brother who wasn't his big brother, driving through *I Am Legend*-land, I became keenly aware of how little I really knew about him. Nearly nothing. Just that he was my age and loved football and that we got along.

Yazid turned toward me. "Moussa got expelled from school today. That's why we arrived so late to pick you up."

"On God's head," Moose protested, "I didn't do anything."

Yazid rolled his eyes.

"Okay, look," Moose said. "A friend got sick and couldn't go back into the school. I had to take care of him, so we skipped out."

"A *friend*?" Yazid said, staring down Moose in the rearview mirror. "Anyone I know?"

Moose didn't answer.

"Use your head, *jeune*! You're on probation already."

"On probation?" I asked.

"At school, yes," Yazid said. "He punched out one of his classmates last fall."

"The punk stole my bike!" Moose said, but I was thinking, Moose? On probation and a brawler? What else didn't I know?

"The principal knew who did it," said Yazid. "You would have had your bike back, no fuss. Instead, the principal called your father. How did that work out for you?"

Moose was quiet.

"Lucky for you, he called me instead of your father today. Getting expelled for two days would be the least of your worries. It'd be back to the *bled* for you."

"The *bled*?" I asked.

"Back to the sticks," said Yazid, as much for Moose's benefit, to emphasize the point, as for mine. "Algeria, to his father's village in Khabylie."

"No gangbanging there, I imagine," I said.

"No football," Yazid said, "no university—nothing to look forward to but tending orchards and sheep. Is that what you want?"

"It's your choice," I said, "either gangbanging or the *bled*."

"Gangbanging?" Moose said. "Stop, okay. I'm not in a gang. I beat up a kid, that's all."

I could see he was kind of pissed at me too, but I didn't care. I was just relieved to know he wasn't someone I didn't know.

"But you're right, Moussa," Yazid said. "Let's not spoil Matt's arrival. You and I will continue this conversation later."

Yazid pulled the car into a parking lot in the middle of the high-rise projects. I recognized them as the ones I'd seen from the window of the RER train heading into town from the airport, and they were even worse up close. A sort of metal-and-concrete ghetto, dingy white and gray cubicle apartments one on top of the other, laundry hanging on lines from windows, satellite TV dishes in place of potted plants. There was graffiti all over, on walls and benches. Here and there a gangly, leafless tree.

"Villeneuve, *mec*," Moose said, smiling. "Home."

MATT

Yazid, Moose and I crossed a big cement courtyard with a fountain that had a rusting sculpture in the middle. "We'll swing by the team clubhouse," Moose said. "Yaz lives there. Then we'll take you to the stadium."

The clubhouse was a ground-floor apartment in one of the high-rises: a long living room with a conference table in the middle and chairs lined up on each side. In one corner was a kitchenette; in another were stacks of boxed gear—hip and thigh pads, jerseys, pants.

A group of guys my age greeted us as we entered. Most of them were black or North African. I rarely noticed that kind of thing, but I did then, and I found myself feeling uncomfortable. Out of place, maybe even a little unsafe. They were all sort of Wu-Tang Clan, straight out of that old "Method Man" video, bandannas around their necks, tuques on their heads. They flocked around me, clapping me on the back.

"This is Matt," Moose said, and they all settled down.

The first to properly introduce himself was pudgy and dark as coal, and he shook my hand old-school soul-brother style. "Me Mobylette," he said with a thick African accent. "Me play running back."

"Mobylette?" I said. It means "scooter."

"He runs faster than one," Moose explained.

"And is squat like a Vespa," another kid added, and everyone laughed.

"I'm Jorge, with a *J*," a gigantic kid said. "I'm your center. Moose says you can throw the ball the length of the field."

"A hundred yards? Maybe not," I said. "But sideline to sideline, definitely."

"Moussa says he'd be the starting receiver on your team. Is that true?"

"Ha! I'd make sure he didn't catch too many splinters riding the pine."

They laughed and ribbed Moose—although, frankly, he was as good a wideout as any we had at school.

It went on like that, soul-brother handshaking and fist-bumping and me answering questions.

"Have you ever been to an NFL game?"

"No, just the CFL, but plenty."

"Are you staying in Villeneuve for the entire season?"

"I hope so."

One of the North African kids said, "*Eh oh*, your accent is too much, *mec*!" He started in, mimicking Céline Dion as a way to mock me—"*Moé, j'te dis que je l'aime en tabarnak, mon ostie chum. René est peut-être un vieux crisse, mais y'a toujours été là pour moé…*"

"*Ouèche, mec*! *Z'y va*! *Vous êtes ouf ou quoi*?" I shot back, mimicking them. "Your accent is pretty unique too." I found myself feeling defensive, and I wasn't usually touchy about things like this. "And by the way, my French and yours are as different as UK and US English."

Fatigue had kicked in suddenly—jet lag. I asked Moose, "Where's the bathroom?"

He pointed to a door. I locked it behind me and stared at myself in the mirror. "What are you doing?" I asked my reflection. "What are you doing *here*?"

I recognized that I wasn't any better than the concierge had been earlier. She'd been suspicious of Moose and Yazid because of the color of their skin, and here I was, reacting just the same with all these guys in this strange place. I felt ashamed, but I couldn't help it. I put my face under the faucet and let the cold water run, the words echoing in my head: *What are you doing here? What are you doing?*

» » » »

When I walked out, Yazid was talking to a tall guy with salt-and-pepper hair who was dressed in a suit and tie. (He was white, and I hated that I found relief in this.) The others had gone, except for Moose, who sat on a chair in the kitchenette, his head slumped forward. Yazid was telling the older man, "I've set up an appointment with the principal at six. If you can join us."

Moose jumped up when he saw me. "This is Marc Lebrun," he said, cutting into their conversation, "our team president."

The man turned to me. "Welcome to France." His grip hurt my hand. He offered me a chair at the conference table. "Moussa tells me you might be interested in joining our club."

The job interview part had started. "I love playing," I said.

"And you seem to be pretty good at it, from what I've been told." Monsieur Lebrun lit a cigarette. "If we can work things out, maybe you'd be interested in also coaching some of our younger players."

Coaching? I'd watched my dad my whole life. "I'd love to," I said.

Moose took a seat beside Yazid, who was sitting beside Monsieur Lebrun. Monsieur Lebrun began describing the Diables Rouges organization and the team's financial sponsors, who paid for player insurance and other related expenses; I wasn't sure why he was telling me all that stuff.

"You're eighteen?" he said.

"In three months."

"So we'll need your parents' written permission."

"Of course," I said, kind of winging it. "While I'm here, my cousin acts as my guardian."

"Your cousin?"

"Juliette. I'm staying with her." The look on her face earlier had made that seem like an increasingly remote possibility, but I had to tell him something. "Well, until I can find a place. You know—a dorm or a hostel or something. I'm sure she can fill out whatever forms need to be signed."

"We met her today," Moose said. Then to me, "You'd probably do better to just email the forms to your father."

Shut up, Moose, I thought.

"And she's your guardian?" Monsieur Lebrun said. "Your legal guardian?"

"Yes, sir," I lied.

Monsieur Lebrun pulled hard on his cig. "But you won't be staying with her?"

"I could," I said, "but she's real busy, you know. Finishing her doctorate. I don't want to be a distraction. And her place is tiny."

Monsieur Lebrun looked from me to Moose and back again.

Yazid jumped in. "He could stay here with me. The couch folds out."

That crappy old thing? I thought. My bed for the next four months?

But I said, "That could be a great option!" You know, to sustain the lie.

The door flew open, and two North African girls around my age came in. Both wore baggy jeans and oversized long-sleeved T-shirts with bright-colored headscarves. They looked anything but traditional.

"So where's our new coach?" the first one said.

"Mathieu, meet our flag-team captains," Monsieur Lebrun said. "Aïda and Yasmina."

"The team's co-ed?" I said.

"That's right," the first girl shot back, "and two *girls* are the captains."

"Don't be surprised," Yazid told me. "They are my two best players."

"So you're the Canadian superstar?" the first girl said, sizing me up.

"I'm no superstar," I said. "I'm just here to play."

"Well, why hire him then," she said to Monsieur Lebrun, "if he's just average?"

"I'm Yasmina," the second girl said. "Welcome." And she got on her toes to kiss me cheek to cheek. "Ignore Aïda," she added.

Aïda turned to Moose. "So they expelled you, too?"

"Leave it alone, will you?" He dropped his eyes away from Monsieur Lebrun and Yazid. "It's under control."

"Under control! Sidi puked all over our living room. My mom's apoplectic, and Dad's sure to whip his sorry butt as soon as he gets home."

The room was silent.

"Come on, Moussa," Yazid said, "tell us what happened."

Moose threw his hands in the air. "All right, all right. Sidi smoked some hash with some guys at lunch and ended up pretty bad, okay. I walked him around the playground, but I couldn't get him back down."

"So you take him home and leave him out cold on the couch!" Aïda said.

"What else could I do?"

"Enough," Monsieur Lebrun said. He turned to Moose. "Why did you get expelled?"

"The doors were locked, so I had to break a window in the gym. A teacher heard."

"Wait," Monsieur Lebrun said. "You got expelled for breaking *into* the school?"

Yasmina giggled, but Aïda said, "On God's head, you're a bigger loser than my brother."

Monsieur Lebrun took one last long drag of his cig, then put it out in the ashtray. "If I'm to get you to your cousin's," he said to me, "and back in time to meet with the principal, we need to leave now."

"Okay," I said. I leaned to Moose and whispered, "That's some craziness, you dumb ass."

"Yeah, yeah," he said. "I hope Marc and Yaz can talk the principal out of calling my father. Otherwise I'm done for."

"It'll be okay," I told him, hoping it would be. Otherwise I was there on my own.

As Monsieur Lebrun and I were leaving, Aïda called after us, "The flag team has practice tomorrow. Come by, and you'll see exactly what girls can do on a football field."

MATT

It took a few days for things to cool off with Juliette. But I'll confess: at first I didn't think they would at all. I thought she'd still see me as the bratty, egotistical kid she used to babysit, and I would have to live out in Villeneuve with Yazid.

And my mom and dad...well, let's just say it took a bit more than a few days, and I had to make some big concessions—mostly about Orford—to get them to sign the permission forms and not fly over to drag me back to Montreal.

The first two weeks I commuted up to Villeneuve, and I had some pretty good practices. It felt great to be suited up and zipping passes! The level of play was really uneven though—more so than I'd imagined. Guys like

Moose and Sidi—Aïda's brother, the one Moose got into trouble protecting—stood out, not for their skill but for pure athleticism. Others looked the part in pads, even if they were a little clumsy. Jorge was bigger than my center back home. But a lot of it was kind of comical. I could see why *US Football* magazine had ranked the team so low.

Still, the guys were super pumped that I was there and excited for our home opener in two weeks, against a team called the Jets from another Parisian suburb. All the guys *really* hated the Jets. I didn't know what the Jets were like, but I hoped we could get by on enthusiasm and guts.

The senior team's season opened that Sunday, the week before our opener—a "friendly" game, as they called them here, against a team from a lower division. It was at home in Villeneuve, so all of us went, the Under-20s, the bantams, the flag team, including Aïda and Yasmina. We all wore our home jerseys, like the senior side. I had to pay off Sidi to get to wear 15 for the season; it was my number back home, but he typically wore it for the Diables. It only cost me bottomless Cokes at the café beside the RER station while we played foosball after practice one night—pretty cheap in the big scheme of things.

The senior team was sixty deep, some with good size; in uniformed rows, stretching before kickoff, they looked good. The three leading warm-up—the QB from the cover of *US Football*, a lineman and what looked to be a linebacker—were obviously North American. You could tell by the way they carried themselves, the easy swagger—though whether they were from the United States or Canada, I couldn't say. The visitors, the Sphinx, were a pretty ragtag bunch by comparison. Some had white helmets with white face masks; others, white helmets with black face masks. A few wore black on black. During their warm-up, they weren't sharp at all. If they had an American on their side, he was disguising it pretty well.

Music blared over the loudspeakers—French hip-hop. I couldn't really make out most of the words. Something like "*J'suis trop ghetto pour cette France...D'où vient le malaise...Trop de différence de rue case nègre à Paris seize...*" The stands were filling up. I noticed this kid six or seven rows up from us, sitting by himself, away from everybody else. He was black but clearly not from here. In fact, he was pretty obviously American, certainly an athlete, probably a football player. He looked wiry but was broad-shouldered, and his neck was too thick for a French player. Safeties back home were built like him (though by the way he carried himself—kind of guarded, uneasy, hands deep in his pockets and hunched into himself in his letterman's jacket—I'd have said he was from the States, not Canada).

I pointed him out to Moose. "From one of the other teams?" I asked. "A scout or something?"

"A spy?" Moose said. He leaned into Sidi, on the bench below us, and whispered something in his ear. Sidi looked up at the kid and shrugged. Moose turned back to me. "Let's go see."

The American turned toward us as we approached.

"You're from the States?" I said.

He gave a slight nod but kept his focus on the field.

I sat down beside him all the same. Moose sat on the other side. "Mathieu Dumas," I told him and offered my hand. "My friends call me Matt."

"Freeman B...," he said. It sounded like Bay-HAN-zin, or something like that.

"Moussa Oussekine," Moose said, and he threw out his hand for a soul-brother shake. All the Diables shook that way; it surprised me at first too, and this black guy, Freeman, was looking kind of suspiciously at Moose for doing it.

The senior Diables kicked off—a good kick, high and deep. Their coverage team tagged the returner, and the American was like, "Oh, dang!"

"Fabrice, there," Moose said in English, "is the most hard hitter on the senior side."

"That was not particularly friendly," the American said in French, "for a 'friendly' game." His French was a little stiff, and he had a heavy accent. Still, you had to like the effort.

"The French are odd that way," I told him. "They call pre-season games 'friendlies,' as though guys in plastic armor ramming into each other could ever be warm and fuzzy."

"You are not French?" he said, using the formal *vous* for me instead of *tu*.

"Canadian. From Montreal," I responded in English.

"But you"—*vous* again—"reside here?"

"For the season. I play on the junior team. I'm going to coach a bit too."

He looked surprised. "Junior like JV?" he asked in English.

"The Under-20 division. One of fifteen or so clubs, across two divisions. It's club teams here," I explained, "not affiliated with schools like back home, so no varsity and JV."

"They pay you to do it? To coach and play?"

"Insurance, an allowance for my cousin who boards me and for my meals and subway fare."

"Nice gig," he said.

On the field, the senior Diables had the ball and were driving toward the end zone. They were methodical—a dive that gained four yards, a sweep that went for eight.

Freeman turned to Moose. "You too?" He kept to English.

"No, I am French."

"French? Right," he said a little snarkily. "But what I'm asking is, they pay you to play?"

"Ha! This is only for the foreign 'talent.'" He reached across Freeman and nudged me. "To keep this one from getting too sick for home and running back to his *maman*." Then he put his fists to his eyes and made a *wah-wah* crying gesture.

I shoved him, and he slapped at my hand, but Freeman leaned out from between us, a little peeved, and we stopped. "So is it the regular season over here right now then?" he asked.

"The French have to do everything their own way," I said, for Moose's benefit more than to answer Freeman's question. "They play January to April here."

"Hear tell y'all Canadians ain't so different, doing things your own way." I hardly understood his English. "Three downs instead of four, twenty-yard end zones, playoffs in October..."

"And not just with football," I said. "Here, they call hot dogs *ott doe-gue*." I pronounced it like Inspector Clouseau would. "In Quebec, we call them *chiens chauds*."

Literally *hot* and *dog*.

"Like a little Dachshund puppy in a bun," he said, "steam rising all up off him."

And he and I laughed.

Moose didn't. He looked like he couldn't follow what we were saying. He said, "I will be honest, my teammates and I"—he pointed to our guys, who were all looking up at us—"we thought that maybe you were a spy from the Jets."

"A spy? Ha! Before yesterday I didn't even know y'all played here."

"Do you play?" Moose asked him.

"Yeah. Back home."

"I could tell," I said, in French to make sure Moose could stay in the conversation. Freeman wore a gaudy ring—a school ring, I'd thought at first, but maybe it was a championship ring. "Where's home?" I asked him.

"San Antonio." He said it kind of boastfully.

"They say Texas high-school football is the best."

He gave me a long look, as if to say he couldn't believe I would actually question this. "Sho nuff," he said finally.

The cocky bastard.

Then Moose said in English, "Maybe you would desire to play for the Diables Rouges?"

Freeman didn't respond; he just stared back at Moose, face blank, clearly surprised. And I remember thinking, Sure, why not? Like me.

If he was for real, that is.

Moose said, "What age do you have?"

"Seventeen."

"*Parfait*," Moose said.

Freeman looked Moose up and down, as if he wasn't taking him seriously.

"Why not?" I said. "Under-20 teams can field two foreign players. We only have me."

"I start college at the end of January," Freeman said.

"Postpone until the fall," I told him. "That's what I'm doing."

Moose looked more and more excited by the prospect of it.

"Playing football in Paris," I said. "How many opportunities like this do you think you'll get? I mean, if you think you could make the team, that is."

"I'd own this league!" Freeman said.

I got up, and Moose followed. We started back down the bleachers.

"We practice here tomorrow at six," I told Freeman. "Come by. Let's see what you've got."

FREEMAN OMONWOLE BEHANZIN

Finding out about the game had been a complete fluke. I didn't know that Villeneuve even existed, much less that they played football there. I'd come upon a poster in the metro the day before. It had a picture of a running back, a buff Brother, straight-arming a would-be tackler, some high-rise buildings off in the background, *Match Amical de Football Américain* block-lettered along the top. And I was like, *For real?*

But sitting on the RER train headed back into the city after meeting Matt and getting the Arab's invitation to try out for the team, I knew there was no way I'd go back up there the next day—no way!—'cause I had to get home to the States, to Mama and Tookie and Tina. Then to Iowa State. There wasn't no way I could stay longer in France, so why even mess with it? Still, the whole ride back, my mind kept troubling the possibility of it.

» » » »

My host family's building, by the Parc Monceau, was fly: marble floors and fancy ironwork on the windows and doors. Their apartment was bigger than our whole house back in San Antonio.

When I walked in the door, Françoise, the mom, called from the kitchen, "Just in time. Dinner is almost ready."

In the family, there's Françoise, Georges, the dad, and a daughter named Marie, who is away at college. Georges was sitting on the sofa, listening to the news on this old-school transistor radio, holding it up to his ear, the volume turned low. He clicked it off and asked me how the game was.

"*Merveilleux*," I said.

"You see, Françoise?" he called toward the kitchen. "I told you it would be fine."

I had told him and Françoise that the game was a class excursion because they had been worried about me going up to Villeneuve. "It is a very dangerous neighborhood," Françoise had said, looking grave, when I'd asked where to find it on a map. Me, I was like, *Paris, dangerous?* But Georges had chimed in, all serious too, "People don't go there."

I thought, Well, somebody must, because folks live there. I had seen the poster.

But Georges wasn't all wrong. Villeneuve, when I first stepped out of the RER station, was *not* Paris. For real. Not like the Paris I'd been getting to know anyway. The train dropped me next to some projects—straight-out-of-the-hood projects. Jacked-up cars on cinder blocks, tagged-over concrete and steel. Everybody hanging about was colored folk, like me: African and Arab, a smattering of Asians. White folks too, but they blended in, carried themselves like the rest.

The place was more Arab than not though. On the boulevard beside the station was a bunch of boutiques and stands, bustling, their signs in Arabic. Men in suit coats and shirts but without ties stood on the sidewalk outside. Most had mustaches and were hawking everything from gold necklaces to cameras. Inside, the stores were full to bursting with shoppers, mostly women, some veiled, all with kids, coming and going through the glass doors.

Georges walked to the kitchen door. "You worry for nothing, Françoise," he said in thick-accented English (even though the host families were only supposed to speak French around us). "I told you his teacher would see to his well-being. The Americans are good and trustworthy people too, after all."

Georges is straight up the class clown. From day one, he'd been picking at Françoise, acting like she was neglectful or inconsiderate toward me, or just one of those snobby French types that doesn't like Americans (which she is not, not none of it!—she's the sweetest lady I've ever met). He'd act like he had to take up for me. At breakfast he'd say, "Voyons, Françoise! The sugar bowl—it is empty. The Americans are good people, are they not? Shouldn't they have sugar for their coffee too?" (I didn't ever even drink coffee.) If she didn't refill my plate lickety-split, Georges would scrunch up his face in a put-upon rage, like it was him that had been wronged. "Ah, no! We must feed this poor boy properly. The Americans are good people too!" Françoise would just wave him off and keep on with whatever she was doing, but I always busted a gut behind his antics.

The day I went up to the game in Villeneuve was a Sunday, and Sunday meals had been a big deal the two Sundays I'd been here, but that night seemed different. Special. Françoise set out the nice china and silverware they had used at the meal when I'd first arrived, and after salad, she served *coq au vin*. It's just chicken, but stewed in this wine sauce, and I'd told her I loved it the first time she made it. She brought it from the kitchen with a fanfare like, *Ta-da!*

Georges leaned forward in his chair as he served me. "It is really a pity that you are returning to America so soon.

Marie has holidays soon. We will meet her at Mont Blanc. The *Alpes françaises*!"

I asked, "How many years have you been to make to ski?"

I could always hear it when my French was slipping.

Georges continued in English. "Me, since I was this high." He indicated his knee with the flat of his hand. "I am really quite expert. Marie too. As for Françoise..." He wobbled his hand on the air. "*Comme çi, comme ça.* She's so-so..."

She slapped his arm.

"And you, dear boy," Georges said, "do you ski?"

In San Antonio? Right.

"If you were not leaving, then you could accompany us!" He was all excited-like.

"Yes. That is kind to say," I said.

"So, how was the game of *foot* you and your classmates went to see?" Françoise asked.

I knew she meant soccer. "Very interesting," I told her. "But it was football."

"Football?" she said and made a kicking motion.

"*Le football américain*," I said and mimed a catching motion with my hands, though I expect she didn't know what this signified.

"*Le football américain*?" Françoise said. "I didn't know it was played here."

"But of course it is, my love. Americans are good people too, *n'est-ce pas*, and like we French, they need sports to distract them from life's more serious affairs."

We went back and forth like that in French (well, me and Françoise anyway). See, I got French like a skunk got stink. Natural. That's why Ms. Glassman, my teacher, took to me: 'cause I was the only jock in her class, and I be *cooking* with my French. For real. I hadn't even considered trying to go on this trip when it was announced at the beginning of the school year. It was Ms. Glassman who called Mama and told her I should apply. She said there was an all-expenses scholarship I'd be a good candidate for—and I got it!

The two weeks here had flown by. Ms. Glassman led the group of us on daily excursions: the Louvre, Notre Dame, all what you'd expect. Interesting. Me, typically I'd bounce as soon as we were free. Not snobbish or nothing, it was just that none of the others in the group really appealed. They were three guys and eight girls. Most of them I knew by sight from the hallways at Heritage Park, our high school, and they'd be friendly enough. But they'd be all loud all the time, always wanting to stay just among us, never with the French, and they'd always be speaking English.

And all of them were white. I hadn't thought it would matter before coming, but I felt like a fly in buttermilk the whole time I was with them. They'd always speak *at* me, never *to* me. Whenever we were together, the white boys would break into some funky pseudo-ebonics, like I wouldn't understand if they spoke proper. One or the other would toss out knuckles; he'd be like, "Whaddup, bruh!" or "How's it hanging, cool," all but calling me "my nigga."

"*Bonjour*," I'd say back. "*Ça va bien, merci*"—It's going well, thanks—and offer my hand to shake like the French do. For real.

Back home, I talk like I talk, not 'cause I don't know better but because I *do*. Mama corrects me, but with my boys, how I talk is who I am. These here on this trip weren't my boys, and whoever they thought I was, I wasn't. So I would throw my French at them and keep my distance and bounce from the group whenever I could.

I'd walk around. The Latin Quarter. The Bastille. Les Halles. Sometimes I'd stop in a café and have a Diabolo Menthe (mint syrup in *limonade*, which isn't lemonade at all but more like a French version of 7-Up) or a Monaco (*limonade* but this time with a red syrup called grenadine). I'd watch folks, the passersby or those drinking wine at the bar and chatting with the barman, or the clusters of college students at the tables outdoors, even in winter, smoking cigarettes and talking and laughing.

Those would be my days. A great trip. Nothing like I would have expected and a diversion from all that was happening back home. That coming Wednesday, me and the rest were set to go back.

After the *coq au vin* (I had seconds!), me and Georges and Françoise moved to the living room for dessert—a strawberry tart that looked awesome, the glazed fruit in spiral rows on top of a yellow cream filling. Françoise brought in a tray with a stack of small dishes on it—and also Champagne glasses. She sat on the settee beside me and began slicing the tart, but Georges left the room, and when he came back, he was carrying a bottle of Moët and a saber, and I was like, *A saber?*

He stayed standing, all formal and serious, so that it didn't fit. "In France, we toast important occasions with Champagne," he said in French. "Today is special for us, for we have welcomed into our home a person who has touched us most deeply."

And I remember thinking, Is he talking about me?

Françoise was standing beside him then, all smiles, and he went on. "We have only known you, Freeman, these few weeks, and we know that in many ways it must be a difficult time for you, to be away from your home. But during this time you have become a son to us. We hope we have been family for you too."

I didn't know what to say.

"*Merci*," I said. "*Merci*." And I meant it.

Georges, still all formal, took that saber and, holding the Champagne at the base, ran the saber in one fluid swoop along the bottle from bottom to top. There was a *clink!* and the head—cork, surrounding glass and all—just popped right off, straight up, and hit the ceiling. Foaming liquid bubbled out, and I couldn't help myself. I blurted, "Oh, *merde!*"

FREE

I didn't hardly sleep that night, partly because of the Champagne, but it was more than that. A dream woke me up at, like, two, and I never got back to sleep after. I still remember it. There was a huge stadium, and no light but that from the moon. The whole scene, it was more *Lord of the Rings* than Super Bowl. The stands were packed with trolls and muscled-up dwarves, humans too, but all gnarly and greasy-haired, the whole lot of them in leather tunics and waving giant swords and battle axes and such, standing and roaring at each other, one army on one side and folks from the other army opposite, some invisible dividing line keeping them apart. Who knew what was at stake? I didn't. All I knew was that I was in a mass of folks I didn't know, hating them others over there.

I can't remember how this came to be, but a small group of us—five or six—were sneaking through the passageways under the stands, by where the concessions and restrooms should be, concrete corridors and pipes overhead dripping water and hissing steam, because we realized—suddenly—that we were on the wrong side, that ours was the one opposite us. And besides, the whole thing seemed kind of ridiculous—all the beefing and posing that none of us could make sense of. Working our way to the proper side, we decided to just find the exit instead, to get on out and away from all the madness.

But then someone from the stands spotted us. He pointed, and raging folks started streaming down the exit ramps toward us. We broke away, running as fast as we could down the long concrete corridors. They overran one or two of us right off, but I got out into the open, onto an empty parking lot, headed for the gates. They were fast, but I was faster. But then there were some in front of me too, coming suddenly out of nowhere. I thought I could deke them—I hoped I could—and then everything went black.

I remember thinking that was the end of the dream, that I was awake. But when my eyes snapped open, I wasn't in Marie's room, where I'd been sleeping, but back in the stadium, in the middle ground between all those folks raging and roaring at each other, and now they were all—both sides—roaring at me. I couldn't move;

maybe I was trussed up or something. I couldn't even turn my head from side to side. I just stared straight ahead. Then somehow my view of the scene panned back, and I could see it from above. From there I could see that my head was chopped off and on a stick, dripping blood and dangling ragged strands of neck meat! And I was screaming...

There wasn't any more sleeping after that. But it wasn't just the nightmare that kept me up. It was my thoughts churning. I just lay there in the dark, looking around the room—at the chest of drawers that stood against one wall, at the sink in the opposite corner—and I couldn't stop myself from thinking about home and why I had left.

I had found out about getting the France scholarship the same week I signed the letter of intent to play at Iowa State: at the end of November, right before Thanksgiving. The recruiter came to our house in San Antonio with my coach, Coach Calley. It was the recruiter's third time over, and he told me and Mama about the academic programs at the university and about my good prospects of starting early, and he laid the papers out on the coffee table and set a fancy pen over top of them. He gave me a maroon Cyclones cap once I'd signed.

Mama closed the door behind them after they left, and no sooner had the latch clicked than she started jumping up and down and clapping her hands. Tookie and Tina came out from the back, and they were pogoing too.

I'm not even sure they knew exactly what it was they were carrying on about. Me, I couldn't help myself—I pumped my fist in the air.

"I'ma be a college baller!" I said.

"I'm *going* to be a college baller," Mama corrected me, but she was steady pogoing in place.

"We've got to call your father," she said, and she went over to the PC on the card table in the corner. Mama sat in the chair and Skyped him while me and Tookie and Tina scrunched around her, squatting beside her so as we'd all fit in front of the webcam.

Pops' face filled up the screen, the collar of his camo fatigues framing the bottom border. He was in Iraq, his third deployment, this time at Joint Base Balad, outside Baghdad; he worked on jet engines. It had to have been, like, three thirty in the morning over there, but a couple of soldiers were playing Ping-Pong over his shoulder.

Pops looked like he knew what was coming. His mouth moved before the words could catch up. "So how'd it go?"

"Just great," Mama said, and she started to explain about the full ride and about the engineering program being nationally ranked, but Pops cut her off. "Let the boy tell it, Verna!" Even all grainy in the webcam, and in the weak lighting of the Quonset hut, his face was lit up. The corners of his mustache seemed pushed up onto his temples, so broad was his smile.

"Coach Horton, the recruiter, said they're graduating three corners and a safety," I told him. "Ain't nothing but two sophomore corners and a redshirt freshman on the whole squad."

"There *aren't* but two sophomores," Mama corrected me.

I knew how to say it proper, but saying it like that for Pops seemed right. See, football was always me and Pops's thing. I'd been balling since I was "knee-high to a pup," as he'd say, and before the war Pops would come to every game. He'd grade my play. *Good stick on third down*, or, all stern-like, *You're slacking on kick coverage*. That kind of thing. Pops would be scrutinizing every detail.

He hadn't really seen me play since I'd grown into my chest and college recruiters had started coming around, so I wanted to catch him up as best I could.

He said, "So you've got a good chance to play your first year?"

"Yes, sir," I said. Tookie had gone back to his room, to play Game Boy or some such, but Tina's tiny hand was steady holding mine, and she was smiling Mama's smile. "Especially if I enroll in January and go through spring ball."

"You got the credits?"

"Sure enough. *And* a three-point-six GPA."

Mama said, "My Freeman's going to get to go to university!" Then she added, "What a week. First the award to take the trip to France, now this."

I pulled the brim of the Cyclones cap even lower over my face, told Pops about the scholarship, not bragging, just saying.

He moved in closer to the camera, his face blocking out the Ping-Pong game, like he could reach on through, put his hand on my shoulder. “Son,” he said, “you’ll make the Cyclones a better team and get to go to college, something your mama and me, your aunts and uncles, never got a chance to do. Boy, you are going places.”

My school group had the day free, what with us having just two days left, and I decided to walk to the places around the city I had liked best. The loud-honking and lively Champs-Élysées first. Then over by Montparnasse: gray stone walk-ups and lots of bookshops and cafés everywhere. After that I took the metro to Montmartre, to the Sacré-Cœur, the white stone church that looks like those pictures of the Taj Mahal.

It was cool out but not cold; I was fine in just my Huskies letter jacket. I sat on a green wooden bench in the park at the base of the long staircases that led up to the church. The parks here aren’t parks the way I know them. They’re mostly gravel-covered paths, and the grass is off-limits. Guards in two-toned blue unis with blue box-hats blow whistles at you if you step out onto the green. Still and all, these ladies—young moms and African nannies and Swedish au pairs—brought their kids. The kids were overdressed—in coats and scarves and knit hats—for a winter that seemed like it wouldn't ever come. They freed themselves and ran and made a ruckus like Tookie and Tina would if they were here. The ladies, pushing the empty strollers, followed behind, picking up the cast-off clothes.

I flipped open the paperback that Ms. Glassman had given me: *A Moveable Feast*. She thought I'd like it, and I did. In it, Ernest Hemingway, this writer we read for English, remembers his time in Paris in the twenties, before TVs and Game Boys and such, when he wasn't but a couple of years older than I am now and trying to be an author. Romantic times.

Sitting there, the book open but not reading it, I got to thinking about when I had told my boys—Ahman, Jamaal and Juan—about Iowa State. It was the day after the recruiter's last visit, and we were sitting on the back of the bench at the bus stop on the way to school, our feet on the seats. I didn't say anything, just pulled the Cyclones cap out of my book bag and put it on—sideways, cool-like.

My boys popped up off the bench and tossed out high fives and jostled me.

"For real?" Jamaal said.

"Big 12 football, that's sick, ese!" said Juan.

I had made All-District the year before, and ever since, my boys, all my teammates, expected me to represent at the next level, for the team, for our school. Huskies pride. And it felt good to step up like that—it did, for real.

I put the Cyclones cap back in my bag. Ahman must have sensed there was something else. "What about UT?" he said. "What about wearing the burnt orange?"

UT—the University of Texas—is a factory for NFL defensive backs.

Ahman played corner opposite me, and me and him had been balling together since Pop Warner. Even back then we'd always be jawing about going pro, picking off Tom Brady in the Big Show. But after recruiters started coming around, standing in a group in the bleachers, asking after me, well, we got to thinking that maybe it wasn't just empty boasting.

Still, I said, "How'm I gonna pass on a full ride for a *chance* at a scholarship?" I added, "A bird in the hand," like if I parroted Pops maybe I'd actually believe it like Pops wanted me to.

Juan got my back. "True that. Beats two in the bush." Him and me were co-captains. He was our rush outside backer, all bull-necked and broad up top but narrow-hipped and long-legged. "My papa had a chance to train for TAC resource management." His pops was air force too.

"Woulda meant a promotion to senior master sergeant, but we'da had to transfer out to some base in South Dakota, and he just said no."

"For real?" I said. "Your pops is separating?"

"As of next summer."

And I remember thinking, Dang, I wish my pops would quit the military. I had that exact thought right then, like an omen.

Across the street, there was a line outside Lulu B's taco trailer, like always, construction workers in jeans and boots mostly, their big mud-spotted Ford F-250s lining the road. One's hard hat was camouflage, to look like a military helmet.

"But rising in the ranks," Ahman argued, "being the best he can be, ain't that why he joined in the first place? Ain't that what we're all supposed to try to do?"

And I knew that was true too. Working hard to live my dreams.

Jamaal, one of our receivers (when he actually got a chance to play, that is), jumped in. "Iowa? For real, Free?" He was snickering. "That's the bunghole of America."

They busted out laughing, all Fat Albert, arms and legs pumping the air.

Jamaal was Dumb Donald if ever there was one.

"Man, how you know Iow-a from Iow-bee?" I told him. "You can't even read a map."

"Ooh, snap," he shot back. "You really busted on me there."

And they all kept yukking it up. My boys.

But Jamaal was right. Ames, Iowa? Seriously?

"For real, yo," Ahman said, insistent. "A chance at UT is still a chance, man. More than most get. Be all you can be, Free. How you not gonna try?"

Juan cut in. "Whatever, y'all. If you two," he said, pointing his carrot-thick finger first at me, then Ahman, "don't step it up on Friday night against the Connally QB, won't none of this mean nothing no ways." Then, just to me: "Coach Calley will have your cojones, Iowa State will revoke their scholarship, Ms. Glassman will kick you off that trip, and you'll end up bussing tables over at Gabriella's Taqueria 'cause won't nobody want to know you no more no how."

It was supposed to be motivational, I guess.

But he was right. We were playing Pflugerville-Connally the upcoming Friday for the chance to make the playoffs, and the Cougars were for real, undefeated and ranked number one in the district. Their quarterback was All-State, headed to play at Purdue. Beating Connally was about me beating their QB.

That's what I was thinking about sitting on that bench at Montmartre, and I kept replaying it on the subway back to Georges and Françoise's. What do I do next? I asked myself.

Enroll at Iowa State, or wait for the fall and walk on at UT, fight for a scholarship?

Up in my bedroom, I put on my sweatpants and running shoes, my letter jacket and a cap to keep me warm. Why shouldn't I go on up to Villeneuve, see if these boys could ball? Why not? It would be just another adventure, like old Hemingway had lived. And I'd have a good story to take back home, to tell my boys about.

FREE

I misjudged the time it would take to get from Georges and Françoise's place to Villeneuve and then had a hard time retracing my steps to find the stadium. When I walked up, practice had already started. There were about forty players and a handful of coaches. Matt, the Canadian I'd met the day before, was in full gear and lined up at QB, directing the offense in shell drill. It wasn't the Big 12; in fact, some bits were kind of slapstick. But it wasn't all bad either.

I watched Matt take a snap and drop back, then slip out of the pocket and take off. Homey thought he could run the rock. And he was wearing number 15—a Tebow wannabe, I was willing to bet.

The Arab, Moussa, saw me on the sideline. He pointed me out to one of the coaches. They jogged over, Matt just behind them.

"Glad you came out," Matt said, taking off his helmet.

He had black hair that fell to his shoulders, a ready smile. He spoke English as easily as French—his English was kind of formal though. He introduced me to the head coach, Coach Thierry, who threw out his hand for a soul handshake, like the Arab had the day before, and I was like, *Tsst. Please.*

But I gave it back all the same. "*Vous pouvez parler en français,*" I told them—You can speak French.

"*Bien,*" the Arab said, but then he went on in English. "Eight interceptions! You had very much a good season."

"*Pardon*?" I said.

"I googled you. I had quite a difficult time guessing the spelling of your family name."

"An African king, eh?" Matt said, kind of smirking.

Pops was born a Compson. "My father took the name Behanzin when he joined the air force," I explained. "After high school."

Matt was steady smirking, like that was funny or something. "You ready to run some drills?" he asked.

I put my senior-class ring in my jacket pocket, dropped the jacket on the sideline and lined up at corner. First we played a two-deep, and I squatted in the underneath zone.

Matt tried to lob a pass over my head, like he wanted to test my springs. I got springs. I picked his pass, took it back the other way.

Play after play, he kept throwing to my side. They had some speed at receiver but no real skill. I made a few more plays on the ball.

We broke into individual position drills. I went with an African brother named Celestin, who was coaching the DBs. He ran us through some hip openers, breaking right and left on his command. Some of the other DBs who weren't directly involved in the exercise tossed a ball around, rugby-style, so I started a tip drill with them. Celestin had the whole group do it.

Then the offense scrimmaged the defense. Without a helmet or pads, I had to watch. I stood beside Celestin and the defensive coordinator, a guy they called Le Barbu—"the bearded one"—even though he was clean-shaven. He and Celestin discussed the best call for each situation, but before making it to the defensive captain on the field, they would look over toward me, to see what I thought or some such. Like, did I agree.

(Later, Matt explained that the junior-team coaches were senior-team players. Even though they were older, most hadn't played the game as long as him and me had.)

At the end of practice, the coaches had us go to the goal line for wind sprints. Matt and the Arab Moussa

(Matt called him "Moose") made a point to line up beside me, and I was thinking, All right then, bring it. But the white boy had jets! The Arab too. I had to work so that they wouldn't beat me, and on the last two, the Arab did.

An older guy who had been watching from the sideline (turns out he was the club president, Monsieur Lebrun) came over when we were done, and the Arab introduced him to me. Monsieur Lebrun led me off from the others, a hand on my shoulder, Matt following behind. "You're obviously a good player," Monsieur Lebrun said. "Plus, you speak French. You could help our coaches. I'm sure Mathieu has told you, we have a good organization and..." He said something I didn't quite get. Then: "You would make a good addition."

And I had an offer, just like that.

A few coaches milled around, acting like they weren't really paying attention to our back-and-forth when it was clear they were. The Arab stood a ways off too, but he was steady looking over toward Matt, like Matt was gonna give some signal of my response, like I was going to make a decision right then, right there.

"Because you are a foreigner, we don't have the right to employ you, of course," Monsieur Lebrun went on, "but we could find you suitable lodgings, with board."

I didn't mention the letter of intent or Iowa State. Instead I heard myself saying, "I am living with a host family in Paris. And I would have to ask the permission of my mother."

He lit a cigarette. "Well, I'm sure we could make arrangements with this family, as we have for Mathieu, if they are willing."

And I wondered if Georges and Françoise would even want me to stay.

"As for your mother—yes, of course." Monsieur Lebrun dragged lung-deep on his cig but blew the smoke straight up into the air, clear of us. "If rules pertain as with our American senior-team players, we will need to make arrangements with your school, or enroll you through the CIEE, for your continued eligibility to play in America."

"The CIEE?" I asked.

"Your American organization for international exchange," he explained, looking at me like I should know this. "But that should be no problem." He smiled and offered his hand. "If you are interested, call me. Mathieu has my number."

Just like that. Two days before I was supposed to leave.

When he walked away, Matt was all conspiratorial-like, leaning in close and whispering, like we would be getting over or something. "Excellent! You and I could tear this league up..."

But all I could think was, Nope, it can't be done. It wasn't my commitment to Iowa State I was thinking about—

or my boys Ahman and Juan and Jamaal at the bus stop, all Big-12 whooping, Huskies pride. I was thinking on Pops.

The air force captain and the chaplain had turned up at our house in San Antonio the night after we'd Skyped with him. Dinnertime. Tookie was playing Xbox, Tina was in the kitchen with Mama. It was me that opened the door. What do you say to a man that tells you a thing like that?

"Are you sure?" was what I finally managed. "I mean, we just spoke to him. Yesterday."

The captain did most of the talking, but not much that I held on to. An IED, all available medical resources deployed, something about funeral arrangements. Mama didn't say anything the whole time they were there.

I held her hand and nodded that we understood, and after they had gone I got Tookie to stop crying long enough to get him to his and Tina's room and into his Spider-Man pajamas. He would kind of groan and swat at my hand as I worked the top over his head. "Let me alone," he said, his eyes watery. Tina had already gotten in bed across the room, in this Huskies gray T that I'd given her—it fit her like a nightgown—and she said, "Tomorrow is fish sticks at lunch!" like she'd already forgotten what we had just learned. And when Tookie jumped up and ran to Mama's door and started banging on it—"Mama, Mama, open up. Please!"—and I had to pull him away, holding him in my arms and shushing him, Tina tried to console him too. "It's okay," she said. "Poppy'll come home when he feels better."

I pulled their bedroom door closed after finally getting them to sleep. I could see a crack of light under Mama's door, but when I knocked she didn't answer.

Matt was still jabbering on as the Diables Rouges cleared the field, folks walking into the locker rooms, some already coming out dressed in street clothes. Most were Arabs, with jeans slung low and in oversized Ts, some wearing hoodies, a few in knock-off letter jackets. And I couldn't help wondering, Was the Arab who planted the IED that killed Pops a kid like me too?

Matt just went on and on. "I've been here almost two weeks, and they've been the best two weeks of my life. No parents, no school, just the City of Light..." He was smiling, like that was what this was about, like running off from your responsibilities was such an all-damn-good and easy thing, the best thing that can happen in your life.

DIABLES ROUGES V. JETS
JANUARY 31

MATT

Our six-game conference schedule kicked off a week after Freeman joined the club, against the Jets from Neuilly-sur-Seine. It was as *un*friendly a game as there could be.

US Football ranked the Jets the top team in the country. Where the Diables Rouges were a mishmash of North African and African sons of resident aliens and illegal immigrants, and of foreigners like me and Freeman, the Jets looked pretty much like their suburb, well-to-do Neuilly-sur-Seine: mostly rich white kids with professional parents from industry and government. (Kind of like me too, I guess, on the parents part—well, the white part too.) The poor/rich, black/white thing added to the bad feelings between the two teams.

The Diables Rouges hated the Jets—just hated them. They also hadn't beaten the Jets before *ever*, which was a big part of the reason why Monsieur Lebrun had decided to hire outside help: Freeman and me.

Our field wasn't much of a field. Freeman called it "the Beach." The only patches of grass were inside the twenties, near the end zones. The rest was like a sandlot, with pebbles and all. In the French Under-20s, teams could only play one foreigner at a time, and foreign quarterbacks only for one half. (They claimed our presence would stunt the development of French QBs because we'd hog all the playing time.) It meant I had twenty-four minutes—two quarters—to make things happen.

And I did. I came out blazing. I threw two scores in the first quarter: the first, a deep flag to Moose; the other, a 5-yard dump-off that Mobylette turned into a 68-yard touchdown.

In the huddle toward the end of the second quarter, Mobylette told me, "*Moi vouloir ballon encore*"—Me want ball again—his French rougher than Freeman's. (Mobylette's real name is Amadou. His family—his parents and something like eight kids—had only recently arrived from Mali, a few months before the start of the season.) It was the first play of what was probably my last drive before I had to sit to let Michel, my backup, "develop."

"*Bientôt*," I told Mobylette—Soon.

Apart from feeding him the ball, I had to find a way to get Sidi back in the game. After Moose, Sidi was probably the best athlete on the team—all five feet nine inches, 160 pounds of him. But he was also one of the biggest contradictions. He was reliable, as long as you didn't rely on him.

Like during that game. He was on early. He caught everything I threw his way, five or six passes, until, with the score 14–0 for us, it was like he realized we might actually win, and the catches began to really mean something. After that, he just bricked. He dropped three passes in a row, including one on third down, a perfect spiral that sailed right through his hands and bounced off his chest. We had to punt.

The Jets kept two defensive backs on Moose and were stacking the box to stop Mobylette. With three minutes left before halftime, I needed Sidi to step up. We all did. We could go into the half leading by three touchdowns.

The guys realized our potential advantage too, and they were fidgety in the huddle, nervous like Sidi, looking off toward the Jets sideline, up at the spectators in the stands.

"Listen up!" I barked.

Everyone snapped to, eyes on me.

"Twins right. Action pass 3-1-4. On two, on two. *Vous êtes prêts*!" Ready!

"Break!" they shouted back in English.

I nodded to Sidi. "This one's for you. Just remember to watch the ball all the way into your hands."

He nodded back vigorously and sprinted to his position in the slot (his show of enthusiasm broadcasting to the Jets where I intended to go with the ball).

I lined up behind Jorge, my center, and started the cadence. "Red 99. Red 99. Ready. Set, hut..."

Sidi jumped offside. The referee blew his whistle and threw a flag.

Back in the huddle, Moose snapped at him, "Get your head in the game!"

"The Canadian said it was on one," Sidi yelled back.

The others grumbled and shifted about. From the sideline, Coach Thierry signaled timeout. "Sidi!" he shouted. "Get your butt over here. You too, Moussa."

"Call your huddle," I told Jorge, and I followed them over.

"What's wrong with you today?" Coach Thierry said.

Sidi started up again. "The play was on one, the Canadian called it on one..."

Moose cut him off. "You're supposed to watch the ball, not listen to the cadence."

"Let's go, *les gars*!" Coach Thierry said. "Pull your heads out of your asses. We have them by the throat. Don't let up now."

The referee tapped his watch. "Thirty seconds left."

Freeman, who had wandered over, whispered to me in English, "You're only as good as your last play." He nodded toward Sidi, who stood there with his head hanging. Freeman seemed to be saying, *Forget Sidi—he's out of it.*

But I needed Sidi. Michel, our French QB, would too in the second half.

Back in the huddle, I used what Freeman had said on the others. "We're only as good as our last play." I adjusted my chinstrap. "So come on!" And to Sidi, who'd been trying to throw me under the bus, I said, "Step up!"

I called the same play as before, but on one this time.

"*Vous êtes prêts*! Break!"

I hit Sidi on the quick slant-in. He juggled the pass at first but tucked the ball under his arm and fell forward, and we gained eight yards.

Second down and two yards to go for a first down.

"You want ball more?" I asked Mobylette, imitating his staccato French.

"Me want ball," he answered.

"Pro left. Inside trap 32."

The Jets showed an inside blitz—the opposite of what I'd expected. I needed to change the play at the line of scrimmage, call an audible to another play so that Mobylette didn't get killed, but the Diables Rouges didn't know how to. We'd never practiced the audible. I called the cadence—I didn't have a choice; it was either that or waste our last time-out—took the snap and handed the ball off to Mobylette.

He broke a first tackle and slipped a second before ramming his helmet into the sternum of the Jets safety. First down, inside their 40.

Mobylette was a natural. And with just a month of American football!

The stands were rocking—only five hundred people, maybe, but all of them stomping their feet and chanting, "*Olé! Olé-Olé-Olé!*"

The Beach didn't have a scoreboard. The ref told me, "Thirty seconds left in the half."

The Jets defensive players were in disarray, sniping at each other. Now was the time to go for the jugular. I called the deep flood pass, an all-or-nothing play that sent Moose and Sidi up the left sideline. It was a sure touchdown if the Jets didn't adjust.

I scanned the Jets defense as I walked to the line of scrimmage. They were showing cover 2, perfect for the call. (I hoped Sidi had seen it too.) I called the cadence, took the snap from Jorge and made a five-step drop. I pump-faked to Moose, who was cutting toward the flag, and launched it toward Sidi, who broke open inside their ten, right where he was supposed to. I watched the ball sail through the air, could hear our players on the sidelines, first "Aahh!" then "Ooooohhh..."

Sidi had dropped the ball.

I looked toward our bench. Coach Thierry was holding his head in his hands. Freeman just shook his back and forth. Then I heard a commotion coming from the other sideline.

Instead of returning to our huddle, Sidi was across the field, in front of the Jets bench, swearing at them. I couldn't make out his words, but their players and fans stared at him, kind of dumbfounded. The refs too. Everyone just stood and watched.

But then someone started laughing, and Sidi really lost it. Utterly and totally. He kicked dirt in their direction, shot them the bird with both hands, grabbed his crotch.

Coach Thierry and Moose rushed over and grabbed him. Aïda had come down out of the stands. They dragged him from the field, Sidi spitting insults all the while, even at our own fans, who were laughing now too.

"Dang," Freeman said when I got to the sideline.

Dang was right.

The tide turned in the second half. The Jets just bullied our defense. Their running back, a strong-legged nineteen-year-old Algerian kid, ran the ball down our throats. (Moose said he was a ringer they'd brought in from the high-rises in Saint-Denis, the suburb next to Villeneuve.) Freeman did his best to limit the damage, but they lined up their American on one side of the field, to draw Freeman over (Moose had googled the kid: he was a wuss receiver who'd graduated high school in California the year before), and then they ran their Algerian ringer in the other direction.

Our 14–0 became 14–7, 14–14...By the fourth quarter, we were trailing by twenty points, 34–14, with only two minutes left. I couldn't do anything about it. I had to watch from the sideline.

"What's wrong with Freeman?" Monsieur Lebrun asked. "Why can't he stop them?"

We were standing at one end of our bench.

"He shut their offense down in the first half," I said. "They figured out he's American. They adjusted."

Monsieur Lebrun kicked an empty Evian bottle. "*Merde!* So that's what our opponents are going to do all season? That's what we're paying for?"

I didn't know what to say.

With less than a minute remaining, Moose called our last timeout. The rest of us huddled around him on the sideline.

"This isn't about winning or losing anymore," he said. "It's about pride. We have to make these rich bastards pay. Tax them a little something for their time spent in Villeneuve!"

I wasn't sure Freeman had understood what Moose said, but he sure acted as if he did. On the next play, the Jets ran a fake to Freeman's side, their big running back an obvious decoy. Poor kid. Freeman tagged him anyway—drove the crown of his helmet under the guy's chin—right in front of our bench. The kid was out cold before he hit the ground, his arms limp at his side, his helmet knocked off and skipping down the sideline.

There were only maybe fifty or so fans left, freezing their butts off on the metal bleachers, but they all popped up, roaring. Even the gangbangers in sunglasses and hoodies who watched from the oak tree at the far end of the field *hooah*ed and cheered.

Flags flew, Jets and Diables Rouges players started shoving one other, and I heard Freeman yelling at the running back, "Fucking Al-Qaida motherfucker!" He had his finger in the kid's face. He was like Sidi had been, like he'd lost his mind!

I grabbed him by the face mask, jerked his face to mine. "What's wrong with you!" I said in English, hoping none of our guys had heard what he'd said, or if they had, that none had understood.

He tried to wrestle free of me, lunging for the unmoving Jet.

"Cut it out!" Moose pulled us apart. "The game is over."

MATT

There's a locker room but no lockers at the stadium, so we had to carry our gear in bulky bags, and the strap was digging into my shoulder. Freeman and I were waiting at the corner to cross the street, on our way to catch the RER back into Paris after our loss to the Jets. It was dark and cold and had started to drizzle. We passed through the Cité des Cinq Mille and Freeman again removed the big ring he wore and put it in his jacket pocket. (Like anyone would want to steal *that*.)

At the RER station, we slipped our tickets into the turnstile, pushed our bags through ahead of us and passed inside. The electric board said the next train would arrive in two minutes, but it barreled into the station as we stepped onto the platform, and we got on. Freeman sat in an empty bank of seats. I sat across from him.

Freeman croaked his French more than he spoke it. "I am with regrets for what I did at the finish of the game," he said.

We usually spoke English to each other, except when we were around French people, so I shifted back. "Forget it," I told him.

But really, it had been bothering me since it happened. Part of me wanted to write it off as bitterness, as just a heat-of-the-moment thing, because of the loss. But it was like he didn't recognize that most of our teammates were North African—"Arabs," as he, like most French people, called them. My best friend on the team and his greatest advocate, Moose, was too.

I wasn't so sure Freeman and I would become friends. It could be kind of hard to like him sometimes.

I said, "But *Al-Qaida motherfuckers*? Really? What's up with that?"

He didn't respond.

"Why just single out the Arabs? Because they're kicking your butts in Iraq?"

"Ain't nobody kicking our butts," he shot back.

"It's time you stopped believing Fox News."

Freeman moved his bag from his lap to the empty seat beside him and stared into the dark outside the window. "Don't mess with me about stuff like that," he growled.

The train dipped from above ground into the bowels of the city. The sound of the wheels on the tracks was a metallic humming. I thought about the Jets. They were the number-one team, so by losing to them we'd put ourselves behind the eight ball after our very first game. We'd need to go undefeated from now on to end up at the top of the final rankings and have any hope of qualifying for the championship game.

Go undefeated the rest of the season? Right. With reliably unreliable Sidi, a spotty defense, a crappy backup QB leading the team for one entire half...

What Monsieur Lebrun had said on the sideline at the end of the game haunted me—about what Freeman and I were supposed to be doing for the team. If we lost again, would he send us home early?

At Gare du Nord station, the car filled up. Normally, this was where Freeman would transfer to catch the metro to take him home, but Juliette had asked him to dinner.

He spoke suddenly. "Can't be but one of us on the field at once."

"Huh?" Sometimes I couldn't understand his English any better than his French.

"There can't be but one of us, either you or me, playing at one time, right?"

"Right," I said.

"We've got what it takes to beat the Jets, that goes without saying. We should run the table all season. But here we are."

"Here we are," I said.

"Well, how about this: what if you and me go both ways?"

I didn't follow him.

"I played running back till my junior year," he said. "I got mad skills. And you'll train with the defense, so you can go in on D. That is, if you ain't afraid to come up and hit a body."

"Ha! I played safety two years in high school."

"That way," he went on, "the half when you can't play QB anymore, you go in on defense..."

I finally got it. "And since we can't be on the field together, you boost the offense." It was smart—a great idea. And he didn't even know our heads were on the chopping block. "I bet it'll fly with the team too."

"Get two full games out of us instead of just one and a half," he said. "If we do that and avoid the M&Ms, we be clean as gasoline. Whoop Jets butt, Mousquetaires, all of them."

"The M&Ms?"

"Mental mistakes," he said.

I couldn't help myself; I cracked up. "Right, of course, Mister Cheap Shot to the Chin, Fucking Al-Qaida Motherfucker!"

Even he had to smile at that. Then he got quiet.

"This is okay, you know," he said.

"This losing?"

"Not the losing—of course not that," he said. "But *this*." He pointed toward the floor of the train. "Being here. Back home, Coach tells you when to pee and how to hold your willy. That's all you ever know—what you're told. Here, it's like we got some say in it."

He'd hit the nail on the head. It was what had made me leave home: so I'd have some say in what I did with my life.

We got off at Cité Universitaire. Across from the Parc Montsouris was a bakery. Freeman stopped. "I've got to bring something," he said, dropping his bulky bag in the middle of the sidewalk for me to watch over. "Can't show up to your cousin's empty-handed. I'm suave like that."

He pronounced it swah-VAY.

Through the window I watched him survey all the selections in the glass case. He came back out carrying a box.

"Fruit tart." He frowned. "That mess is expensive!"

"The cost of being suave." I pronounced it like him, but he didn't laugh.

MATT

Juliette had insisted I invite Freeman to dinner because, as my "surrogate mom" (her words, not mine), she said she was responsible for me and needed to know who I was spending time with. But also Juliette could be kind of starchy. She was twenty-five, and since coming over two years ago to do a dissertation on literary feminism of the 1950s, it was like she was more French than the real French. Anyone who didn't have the appropriate credentials was suspect.

I knocked to make sure we didn't barge in on her getting dressed or anything. "Jules, this is Freeman," I said when she opened the door. "Freeman, Juliette."

"Come in," she said in English. "Welcome."

Freeman handed her the tart.

"Thank you very amicably for the invitation," he croaked. Her English is spot-on, as good as mine, and I had told him so, but he kept going back to his overly formal, very guttural French. And he was struggling. "Mathieu speaks very amicably of you," he said.

Amicably again. Swah-VAY.

Jules chuckled. "It's only because he can't afford not to."

He and I sat on the couch (my bed) while she went into the kitchen to check on dinner. We were silent, kind of awkward. Since Jules's pad had only one bedroom, my room was the living room—it was also the dining and TV room. Freeman had told me his host father was a captain of industry or something, so Juliette's place must have seemed like a closet to him. These tiny Paris apartments were quaint when it was just you and your cousin, out in the world, making it on your own, but having another North American there made it seem like what it really was: former maid's quarters, with drafty windows and three people on top of one another.

"I'll be right back," I told him, and I slipped into the shower closet, closed the door and sat on the commode. Just a few minutes to myself.

» » » »

"*The Second Sex* remains a touchstone text..."

Juliette was preaching at Freeman as I served myself a second helping of lasagna. Her goddess was Simone de Beauvoir.

"She sounds fascinating," Freeman said in English, all flirty.

"Hear, hear." Jules lifted her wineglass.

(She'd served us sparkling mineral water.)

"Never heard of her," I lied and plunged a forkful of pasta into my mouth.

She threw a leaf of lettuce at me. "Dumb jock. You should take some cues from your friend here."

Freeman finished his plate and pushed back from the folding card table we'd set up in the corner. "This is by far the best lasagna I've ever eaten," he said in English, and Jules blushed, and I was like, *Stop!*

I said, "Jules, really, is feminism still even relevant?" I knew this would make her thick.

"Relevant!" She pushed aside her plate, not just thick but fuming, her face suddenly flushed. I could almost see smoke streaming out of her ears. "Take a look around, kiddo. Women's rights have a long way to go before..."

I laughed, and she realized I was pulling her leg.

"I'm the one who was raised by a hardcore feminist, remember?" I said.

"Yeah, but your mom ditched the cause a long time ago to embrace consumerism instead."

And Jules was right. My mom runs the biggest women's magazine in Canada, one that torments women monthly—about their age, their weight, their inabilities in bed, in the kitchen, as mothers. I'm just seventeen, but I've spent so many afternoons with her in her office it's like I have a PhD in women's issues. No joke. I probably know more about cellulite and bacterial vaginosis than some doctors.

I mean, don't get me wrong—I love my mother. I'm just not sure I always *like* her very much.

She left my dad eight months before I came to France, after twenty-nine years of marriage. They met at university, when my mom was a journalism major and my dad was the star running back of the team. They say that if he hadn't blown out his knee, he would have been a lock for the CFL—he might even have made it in the NFL! He became a high-school coach instead, and a good one too. But that's also why my mom ended up leaving him. I guess over the years his good nature and fun personality ended up carrying less weight for her than his lack of ambition.

I lifted my glass of water. "To my one and only mom."

"So, Freeman," Jules said, "what will you do after college?"

"Go pro," he shot back, all bravado.

"It's very rare to play professionally, isn't it?" she said. "I mean, it's probably wise to have a backup plan, no?"

He looked down at his empty plate, kind of sheepish. "*Bien sûr*!" he croaked. Then, in English: "But the NFL would open all kinds of doors. So I could launch myself in broadcasting or the business world or something."

Jules asked, "So you guys won today?"

It hadn't come up until then. Neither of us answered.

"You lost?"

"Got spanked," Freeman said.

"At least you didn't get hurt," she said to me. "Your mom would never forgive me."

Freeman and I were in the tiny kitchen, doing the dishes, when Juliette, who was sitting at the living-room window smoking a cigarette, called over, "She phoned again this morning, you know, after you left. You need to call her back ASAP."

"And you need to quit smoking."

Disgusting habit.

"I'm serious, Mathieu."

I didn't say anything, just dried the dish Freeman handed me and replaced it in the cabinet above the sink.

"What's up with that?" he asked.

"My mom wants me to call."

"But why the big deal behind it?"

I just rubbed and rubbed the washed lasagna casserole with a dish towel.

I'd talked to her three times since arriving. The first time, all she did was scream, "You're a minor, for Christ's sake! You cannot leave my house, much less the country, without my permission!"

The second conversation was even worse. She had called from her office and begun by announcing, "Your father is here with me," and I knew I was screwed. My parents were never in the same room at the same time if they could help it. They only talked through their lawyers.

"Hi, Dad," I said.

He didn't say anything, but I could feel him there.

My mom was pacing back and forth; I could hear her heels clacking against the hardwood floor. I'd seen her turn in circles, like a lion in a cage, a gajillion times before.

"The bank called yesterday." Her voice was icy calm and echoed because of the speakerphone. "Not only do you leave the country without permission, but you steal money to do it?"

I didn't answer right away. I mean, how do you tell your parents that you just want to play ball one last season, that you're tired of thinking about your screwed-up family, that you're tired of living one week at your mom's new penthouse with her new boyfriend and the other with your dad at the old family home while it's waiting to be sold?

"Well," I said, "it *is* my money, after all."

That was when she lost it. I won't even repeat what she said. I mean, I just won't repeat it.

My dad had still not said a single word. The entire time, he never did. It was the worst thing he could have done.

"I just needed to get away," I told Freeman now. "My mom's a hotshot magazine editor, and my older brother and sister have big careers."

He stopped washing and stared.

"I'm good with it," I said. "With the expectations. I just needed a little break first."

"They didn't know you were coming?"

"They do now."

"My man Matt, a runaway!" He laughed. "Am I going to see your mug on the back of a carton of milk?"

"The season's over in April, and then I have my whole life to get degrees and good jobs and to make money."

"Dang, son," he said, "you got big cojones. *Beaucoup* big."

"You're one to talk about the size of someone's cojones," I said. "Acting tough but afraid to go skiing."

"Afraid?" Freeman made a sucking sound through his teeth—*tsst*—something between irritated and dismissive. "Please." He kept scrubbing the salad bowl when it was obviously clean. "It's just bad timing is all. The trip falls right between our game against the Ours and the one against the Anges Bleus."

He'd told me one day at practice that his host family had invited him to go skiing with them in a few weeks but he didn't think he would go. "You can catch the TGV down after the game..." I said.

"The TGV?"

"The high-speed train," I told him. "You can catch it on Sunday and be back by Tuesday. You'll only miss one practice, a walk-through."

Juliette had gone to her room to study. He handed me the salad bowl.

"I used to love family ski trips," I told him. "My mom and dad, Marc and Manon. Sometimes my uncle Pierre would bring his kids—my cousins. We'd be all together, you know. There's nothing better."

"These folks aren't my family though."

"For the next four months they are."

There were no more dishes, but he stood there with the hot water running into the empty sink. I reached over and turned it off.

"Is it about money?" I tried to be tactful. "I mean, I can front you some cash if you need it."

"Naw, it ain't that. They're paying for everything." He wiped his hands on his jeans. "It's just that I should be home, that's all," he said. "Sometimes it feels like I ran off too, like you did. I should be back there, helping out."

If we didn't do better than we had earlier, I wanted to say, he would be home soon enough.

"There'll be time for all that," I said instead, because I was sure there would be. "Time's the one thing we've got lots of."

"Lots of time," Freeman said, suddenly dour. "Right."

» » » »

Freeman thanked Juliette for an *amicable soirée.* She was working on her laptop on her bed. She said goodbye but kind of automatic-like, and he looked deflated.

I walked him downstairs.

"So, you gonna phone your mom?" he said as we stood under the porte cochere.

"Tomorrow."

"You better, man, 'cause family's the most important thing." He crossed the street, calling back, "I'ma be on you about it."

I watched him disappear into the dark alongside the Parc Montsouris.

My mom had agreed to send a letter authorizing me to play, but she didn't say much else. She wouldn't accept my apology. She told me I was enrolling for summer classes at Orford the day I got back. She said she would contact the coach at Laval to let him know my decision. *My* decision? We hadn't talked since.

My girlfriend, Céline, sent a long email. She dumped me. She said she couldn't trust me.

I pulled my cell from my pocket, flipped it open and scrolled down the text messages to the one my dad had sent the day after the last call with my mom. **Make things right**, was all it said.

DIABLES ROUGES (1–1) V. OURS (0–2)
FEBRUARY 28

FREE

Me and Matt, Moose, pushing his ten-speed, and Aïda, our flag-team captain, were walking from the stadium to the RER after practice. They were chatting and laughing and whatnot, Matt and Moose horsing around, exchanging clownish looks and faux-sexy glances. Aïda, in her headscarf, smiled at their silliness. Me, I kept to myself.

It had been a month or so since I'd decided to stay. I was having fun and all—living in France, who wouldn't be?—but I wasn't feeling right either. Not easy, like Matt seemed to be. Homesick maybe. I'd Skype Mama every week, and she'd tell me how she was doing ("Fine") and how Tookie and Tina were doing ("Fine"), and she'd ask how it was with me ("Fine," I'd say). So we were all fine, you know. Still and all, as often as not I just felt off, uneasy.

Me and Matt and them passed by the city cemetery and the humming electrical substation that powered Villeneuve—ten-foot concrete walls topped with barbed wire, skull-and-crossbones and Danger–High Voltage signs all over. There was what they called an "industrial park" nearby. It wasn't much of a park: fenced-in construction sites and giant cinder-block warehouses, most of them vacant. A ways off was a congested highway.

"The A1," Matt once explained to me. "The Autoroute du Nord. It leads to Brussels."

"How do you know these things?" I asked.

"How don't you know them?" he said back.

We had the Ours (French for "bears") coming up on Saturday, a game we should win. The Saturday before, we had stomped the Mousquetaires, 42–0. Mobylette killed. Matt kept calling sweeps and Mobylette would turn the corner and blow by the DBs like they were standing still, his legs just a-churning. The boy could scoot! But it was Matt who won the day, calling the right play at the right time, getting everybody involved and keeping everybody focused even as the game got out of hand. Other teams had foreign players too, but Matt was *on*.

Me, not so much. Coach Le Barbu had me at safety, and I played it as a sort of monster-back—part linebacker, squeezing the line of scrimmage when I saw a run coming, and part defensive back, dropping into coverage. I'd been effective, you know. I'd made lots of tackles. But I hadn't shined, really. Not like Matt. I hadn't gotten a single interception, very few big hits. It rattled my confidence for real, yo. And I hadn't played a down on offense. No need for me to.

We wove our way through the Cinq Mille projects. In the concrete courtyard between high-rises, some older guys—gray-haired, a mix of Arab and black—were playing the metal ball game you see old French guys play in the Tuileries Garden in Paris. *Pétanque*, it's called. That was what I was staring at when I noticed this group of dudes a little ways off: five of the hoodie boys that hung out by the big oak tree at our games. Three Arabs and two Brothers. *Chelou*, Moose called them—suspect, shady. One Brother was passing a plastic baggie to another, accepting some bills from him.

One of the Arabs was hawking on me. "*Qu'est-ce tu mates, toi...*" blah, blah, blah, he hollered my way. I hardly understood a word of his slang, but I got the message still and all: he had seen me eyeing his crew, so he was calling me out.

He moved on me, hard, so I pulled up. Didn't say nothing, but I freed my hands from my pockets. He was spitting his slang, his crew pushing up behind.

The old guys stiffened up, like they knew what was about to go down, but they kept playing. Except one, who scooted off into one of the buildings. I felt Matt and Moose behind me.

Moose stepped forward. "Cool, *mec*, cool." His hand was out toward the hoodie boy. "*Y a pas de problème, là. On va à la gare, c'est tout.*"

There's no problem, Moose was telling him. We're headed to the train station, that's all.

The other hoodie boys stood stone-cold behind their boy, who was all face-to-face with me but silent now, one hand in his hoodie pocket. I had four inches on this fool, and I saw his hand reaching, but I knew my hands were quicker, whatever it was he had in his pocket. It just depended what his crew did when it popped off, and if Matt and Moose could hold their own.

See, I know gangster. Northside Rollers, East Terrace Mafia, Latin Kingz—we got all that in my 'hood back home. These boys here wasn't gangster. All Frenchified and whatnot, they were just playing make-believe.

"*Karim, on va à la gare, c'est quoi le problem?*" Moose was mediating, his hand outstretched.

Aïda too. "Cool, Karim. Cool."

She put her hand on hoodie boy's arm, and he snapped it free. "*Qu'est-ce que t'as, toi!*" he hissed at her—Butt out! What's the matter with you!—and Matt stepped forward. But hoodie boy was steady all up in my face.

One of his crew started to do the dope-smoker giggle. "*Hee-hee. C'est les footballeurs 'Ricains des Diables Rouges.*"

The old men, they'd disappeared. Little kids started to gather around, and two others of his crew had started to giggle too.

But not hoodie boy. Karim, Moose and Aïda had called him.

"*Dégages.*" Karim spat and gave this little nod, like he was dismissing us or some such, letting us pass, and I just steady stood there 'cause I hadn't asked his permission in the first place.

Matt grabbed my arm, him and Moose and Aïda moving on, and Matt said in English, "Come on, Free."

Him speaking English caused the other hoodie boys to burst into giggles again, but Karim kept staring at me.

I was steady staring him down too, my eyes like, *Nigga, I got your name now. Karim. I got you.*

Around the corner, in the parking lot of the next set of high-rises, the little kids buzzed around us, asking if we played for the American football team and would we give them autographs. And now here Moose was, preaching at me in his heavy-accented English: "You just do not understand, *mec*. In a place like this, everything must always be normal." He said *normal* in French—nor-MALL. "How you say? Commonplace. You must act as though everything is commonplace. Some boys are selling drugs, *c'est normal*. A fight begins. *Normal*. It is ordinary, nothing that you react to."

But I was like, *Tsst, nigga, please*. "Some fool calls you out, you got to stand tall. Got to. Otherwise he come calling every day."

Moose swatted at the buzzing kids. "*Allez, allez! Dégagez!*"

Dégager. The same word Karim had thrown at us, in about the same tone of voice, too.

"Yes, yes, of course," Moose said to me, "but you must understand also these guys are often with weapons, and they are looking for trouble. It is better to ignore them and just pass on."

"I *was* ignoring them. Dude bumped up on me."

We'd rounded onto the main street, just up the way from the train station, and as usual there were police vans on each side of the road. Matt called the ones in the white vans the CRS—the riot police. Wasn't no riot going on, so I was like, *Whatever*. But Moose said, "Not this again..." He slowed his pace and put some attitude in his step.

And sure enough, a group of five of them rolled up on us. They wore dark blue jumpsuits and army boots; each had a helmet latched onto his belt and carried a metal baton. One held out a hand toward Moose, another toward me.

"*Vos papiers*."

"*Américain*," I said, but he shot back, "*Allez, tes papiers*," all dismissive.

Moose already had his ID card out. He dropped his bag to the ground, opened it and stepped back. Another cop started going through it. The one on me tapped my bag with his free hand; I dropped it too. Matt opened his equipment bag, but they ignored him. Aïda shoved her hands in her pockets, all attitudinal now, like Moose.

The first cop pretended to inspect our papers, but it was all for show. He was just buying time while his boys rifled through Moose's and my bags. They dropped stuff on the ground, turned clothes inside out. One got a kick out of my helmet, turning it over and over in his hands. It was clear there wasn't nothing for them to find, but they kept on all the same, searching pockets, taking things out and leaving everything all over the sidewalk.

One, off to the side, said to Matt, "*T'es Américain aussi?* What are you doing here?" This cop had a single bar on his shoulder patch—a lieutenant or some such—and acted like he was the ranking officer. His name badge read *Petit*.

"I'm Canadian," Matt corrected him. "*Québecois*."

"From Montreal?" Lieutenant Petit asked.

Matt nodded.

"Great music town!" Petit said, and he looked all excited. "I spent a month there last summer during the jazz festival, visiting my older brother." He started imitating this Quebec accent like Matt has: "*Aw-stee, j'vais passer prendre une bière toute à l'ahr, Kriss da Caw-leese…*"

"Is he a policeman too?" Matt said.

The lieutenant stopped mugging. "*Pardon*?"

"Your brother," Matt said.

"He's a lawyer."

"Well then, he would tell you that cops in Canada aren't allowed to stop people on the street for no reason."

The lieutenant smiled. "*Touché*," he said. "Although we are not in Canada here."

He signaled the others to wrap things up. The one who had our ID papers handed them back, and they all turned and moseyed off, lazy-like, toward their van. No "Sorry," no "Good day." They didn't even replace our stuff in our bags.

"*Alors, on se revoit à mon retour dans quelques minutes*?" Moose said to them—So, the same drill again in a few minutes then, on my way back?

"*Vas-y, petit gars*," one of them snarled. "*Dégages*."

That same word. Beat it, it meant, but harsher like, *Fuck off*.

Moose turned on Matt. "Making new friends?"

Matt ignored him.

Aïda said, "The way the police treat us *Beurs*, this utter lack of respect, tells us all we need to know about where we stand in France."

"*Beurs*?" I asked. I didn't know the word.

"Slang for North Africans," said Matt.

I was supposed to be sympathizing, but all I could manage was, "So I can expect more of this crap every time I'm with you?"

"In Villeneuve, probably yes," Moose said. "Our illustrious minister of the interior, in the newspapers, he called us project residents…*racailles*?"

"Scum," Aïda translated, to make sure I'd understood.

"Yes, this. And he vowed to, uh…how you say… *nettoyer au Kärcher*?"

"It's like what the industrial cleaner does," Aïda said, "with a pressure hose."

Moose said, "You see, after a little child died from a stray bullet, the interior minister vowed to clean out the scum from our neighborhoods. He was referring to the *jeunes de la cité…*"

"The youths from the projects," said Aïda.

"The riot police have been here ever since. More than a year now. To them, Karim and me, we are the same."

We arrived at the station. Matt just stood there, like he was waiting for Moose to say something more or for Aïda to go on expressing outrage, but I just passed on through the turnstile.

"For real," I said, "I'm glad to be leaving this shithole."

FREE

Black folks don't ski—that was all I could think. But there I stood, at the top of a mountain in the Alps, on these long Rossignol skis and under layers of clothes, watching Georges and his friends dash down ahead of me. I guess I led them to believe I could keep up.

Dang, I thought.

Georges and Françoise had postponed their January trip so that I could go with them and their daughter, Marie. Georges's friend Jean-Pierre, his wife, Alphonse, and their two kids, Aimée and Guy, who were Marie's age, had come too. All of them gone now down the hill. Even Françoise didn't wait. I watched them zigzagging a path through the sun-bright powder, leaving a smoky trail that I guess I was supposed to follow.

I pushed off like I saw them do. My zigs and zags were broader, and I bogged down on each turn, sometimes to a complete stop. I would work my skis around, point them downhill and push off again.

Other skiers, in loud-colored one-piece suits and matching helmets, flew by.

I tightened my turns and, pretty quick-like, I picked up speed. A lot of speed. Suddenly it was like I couldn't turn hardly at all, my thighs going tight, burning. And my boot-encased feet bounce-bounce-bounced over the little bumps, the moguls, like Wile E. Coyote in a cartoon.

Straight.

Down.

Hill.

That damn Matt had told me I'd pick it up easy! *Any half-decent athlete does*, he said.

I just laid myself over, the only thing I could think to do. The initial jolt was rough, like getting blindsided on a crackback block (harder than any hit I took against the Ours two days before, when we beat them by four scores). But then the powder was soft, and I was sliding on my back, then spinning in a circle and sliding at the same time, until finally I came to a stop.

Both skis gone. One pole too.

"Nice mustache," I heard in English—MOOSE-tah-sh.

It was Marie, appearing out of nowhere. She was leaning into her ski poles a few yards above me, wearing this yellow ski suit that shaped her form just so. I expect I had a face full of snow or some such. Suave.

"I suppose we should have started you on an easier slope," she said.

"Naw, naw. I'm just one fall away from mastering this run."

She helped me up. "You have never skied before?"

I didn't answer.

"I will teach you. Climb on." She pointed behind her. "Place your feet there."

I did and grabbed her waist, and she skied me to my skis, a little ways down. I clicked my feet into them. She showed me how to snowplow to slow myself, how to squat into my turns. When I was being too cautious, she prodded me by poking my butt with the point of her pole. And in this way, she led me down the mountain.

The entire weekend was dope like that. Georges stayed goofy the whole time, telling stories about previous trips and meals they'd had, about the famous people they'd met on their runs and the really hard slopes they'd mastered.

There was never a minute when we weren't doing something—walking around Mont Blanc to see the classic wooden A-frame architecture of the chalets, or building a fire in the fireplace, or going down to the cellar after board games. We played Monopoly (in the French version, it's the Avenue des Champs-Elysées instead of Park Place) and another I hadn't ever even heard of, Mille Bornes. And we ate fondue. Two pots on little burners sat in the middle of the table, one of hot oil, the other of melted cheese. Everybody strung raw meat on long skewers and cooked it in the oil or dipped chunks of bread in the melted cheese.

I was telling Matt about it at practice after I got back, still excited, while we watched Michel, the backup QB, try to run the offense.

Matt cut me off mid-sentence. "It was a great trip, I get it. Football practice is just not as fun as skiing in the Alps. But come on, Free. We've got the Anges Bleus on Saturday, our first real test since the Jets, and you've got to learn the offensive packages before then. Focus."

But I wanted him to know it all. "And Marie!" I went on, whispering but still emphatic-like now, because I could see Coach Thierry glancing back at us. "She's twenty-one, at college and whatnot. And a real hottie!"

Matt ignored me. "Mobylette," he called, pointing to the spot where Mobylette should be.

Coach Thierry added, "*Vite,* Mobylette, *sinon on va être* offside!"

It was early March, gray and chilly but crisp. The offense was supposed to be in Trips formation, but Mobylette had lined up in the backfield. He scrambled to the right place, and Michel called the cadence. The offense exploded off the snap, but the receivers were all over the place, bumping into each other. Some real Charlie Chaplin stuff.

"*Merde, merde, merde!*" Coach Thierry snapped, frustrated by the bungling. "*Qu'est-ce qui se passe...?*"

He started toward Mobylette. Matt followed, but I grabbed him by the arm. "You think she be trying to mack me, man? A grown woman, jocking me?" It was hard to keep it to a whisper. "Tell me I ain't for real!"

Matt stopped and kind of glared.

"Free, I swear, if it weren't for context, I wouldn't understand half of what you say. You're always jabbering, but I mean, I'm a Francophone, and, strictly speaking, I speak English better than you."

"Different," I told him.

"Different?"

"Different than me," I said. "Different don't equate to better. It's how black Americans speak, how we been speaking since slavery." I was speaking it heavy right then to make my point. "You saying what you just said is like calling me out of my name. Like me saying you was French when you ain't."

"I'm *Québecois*."

"Right. You just speak French."

"Some say a bastardization of it," Matt said. "Some French people anyway."

"Right! But you know you're not lesser on account of the difference."

"Right," Matt said, his face gone soft, apologetic.

"*Alors, les filles*!" Moose called over. "You going to quit with the English jabbering and help us out here?" He looked as annoyed as Matt had just a few moments before.

The other guys had all stopped too. Everybody stared.

» » » »

On the train headed back to Paris, Matt sat silent. Not ignoring me, just not talking. I figured it should be me all mad after what he had said about black English, but he just sat there, stewing.

"You still want to go to that cemetery?" I asked.

Père Lachaise. Jim Morrison's grave. I didn't really want to go, but Matt had been talking it up for days. Apparently lots of hippies hung out there, lots of girls, people passed around jugs of wine, and it was generally a party. Myself, I didn't feel like partying in a cemetery. *Especially* not in a cemetery.

Still and all, I said, "Well, do you?"

"Not tonight," Matt said, and I was straight-up relieved.

The RER arrived at Gare du Nord, my transfer point. When I got up, Matt did too; he walked me toward my metro line and I couldn't figure out why, because the one we had been on led to his cousin's spot. My look must have stated my question.

"I've got an errand to run," he explained.

We sat side by side on the metro but didn't speak. A long silence. I thought I knew what was eating him, and it wasn't just practice. It dated from a little while back. "Look, I'm sorry," I said, "but Villeneuve *is* a shithole. Cops everywhere, wannabe gangsters..."

"When you say things like that, you sound more like a Jet than a Diable Rouge. Your 'shithole' is Moose's home."

"I know," I said.

I watched the dark tunnel walls stream past the window.

"Listen, I like Moose and all, but he rides me. Always tossing out snarky comments and whatnot. He acts like he's got something to teach me, but the kid is seventeen, just like me, and hasn't been balling one-tenth the time I have."

"He's the team captain and wants to be a schoolteacher. For him, everything is a potential lesson or a teachable moment."

"Well, I'm not his pupil, and besides, his teaching method needs work."

"Moose takes the team very seriously. It's his life, you know—community pride and all that. Sometimes you act like you're on vacation."

I *was* on vacation, but that didn't mean I wasn't bringing it for the team. But I didn't say that.

We got to my stop, and I stayed seated. "I already told Françoise I wouldn't be back for dinner," I said. I figured we should hash this thing through, me and him. "I'll ride with you."

"You don't have to."

"Ain't got nothing else to do."

He didn't seem any too pleased, but he didn't protest either.

I felt like there was something more I should say, to kind of make up for something—for how I'd been acting, being moody and all, or for whatever expectations I wasn't living up to. But we just sat there, silent. I didn't know what to say. He didn't say anything either.

He got off the train a few stops later, at Ternes. I followed him down the platform and up the stairs. "How's my girl?" I said to lighten the mood. "Is Juliette asking after me?"

He smiled. "Actually, she is. You made quite an impression."

"I told you so. I'm a killer!"

We got out on the street, and he stopped under the illuminated yellow *M* metro sign and extended his hand. "Okay, killer. Goodnight."

And I was like, *Huh?*

"This is my errand." He pointed to the hotel across the street from the station. "My dad. He arrived this morning."

"Uh-oh," I said. Obviously he'd been brooding over something too.

"He called from the airport and told me to meet him here."

"With no advance warning?"

"Not a word."

"Dang."

"Dang is right," he said.

He had told me how close he and his pops were. He said his pops had made him who he was. He'd taken Matt to rallies and protests: for Earth Day, against global warming, to oppose the US invasion of Iraq (the last hardly surprised me). But Matt said his pops had been different since Matt ran off.

"Juliette didn't give you any clues he was coming?" I asked.

"I don't think she knows he's here. And I haven't told her."

"Not Moose?"

"Just you, just now." Then he smiled. "If it was your father just showed up like this on leave from Baghdad after you'd done something like what I did, he'd be coming to kick your butt, right?"

I hadn't told Matt about Pops. I wasn't thinking I would. I mean, it wasn't none of his business. Besides, Pops had made me a man. I knew that his death was my weight to carry. Mine alone.

I said instead, "I expect your pops is here to make sure you're all right. It's all good. Don't sweat it." I pushed off up the street. "Holler at me tomorrow. Let me know how it goes."

At the corner I turned back, and he was still standing there, facing the entrance to the hotel, strangely lit by the pale glow coming from the lobby—part shape and part shadow, kind of like a ghost. A doorman pushed open the door, and Matt walked in.

Naw, I remember thinking. If it was Pops that had showed up like that, it wouldn't be about scolding me, about calling me out. He'd be about making sure I was good to go. He'd come by a game, and he'd see that I was wearing 49, his high-school number, instead of 17, like I did back home. He'd even help out with the team, the days he was here.

Maybe he'd take an extended furlough, stay the whole season, coach the Diables. And he'd take me around places. Versailles, Normandy, a TGV back to the Alps.

The clock on the corner by Georges and Françoise's building said it was quarter to nine. I sat on a park bench between streetlights in the almost-night, looking up to the lit windows of their apartment. Nine ten, nine thirty-five, nine fifty-five...I waited until the apartment went dark.

When I got upstairs, I snuck quiet-like past Georges and Françoise's room. In my room I took from the desk the letter I'd been writing to Mama. Not email, a real letter—paper and pencil, like in the Hemingway book. I'd been working on it for days—writing a sentence and scratching out another, erasing and replacing words, scribbling in the margins—but now I finally knew how to write it.

I'd known it was cowardly to not go back at the end of the class trip, to not try and help Mama out some way. I did! But I'd also known something felt right about staying. Making my own way, living in Paris, getting to see something more—going places, like Pops had said. And I'd known Mama wouldn't say no to me staying. She hadn't protested about me coming on the trip in the first place. She didn't do anything.

» » » »

Auntie Constance drove in from New Orleans after Pops died, and it was her who called the Army Casualty Program and the life-insurance people and the funeral home. Mama sat on the sofa beside her, silent. After the funeral, everybody who had come in flew out. Auntie Constance took Tookie and Tina back to New Orleans. It was just me and Mama, our house suddenly so empty.

I heated up Hungry Man fried-chicken dinners that first night, even though the fridge was full of leftovers from the buffet at the wake. I told Mama, "It'll take us days to eat through all Aunt Joanie's deviled eggs and the meatloaf and the Hoppin' John that Grandma Jessie left. We'll be okay for a good stretch."

Mama "mm-hm"ed.

There was still all kinds of stuff to get done, filling out forms and whatnot, insurance and pension stuff. I told her, "If you need me to, I can stay back from school. To help out."

She shook her head no and dropped her face, tears shining her cheeks.

I didn't insist. I let it be.

A little while later she came into my room, wearing an old shift and house shoes. "I think I need to go to Connie's too," she said. "Be home in a while."

And I remember thinking, Home? It ain't here?

But I told her, "Yeah, of course. Go ahead. You should go."

She just stood there, framed by my bedroom doorway, eyes sunken, black and heavy. "You'll be fine," she said, "with Ms. Glassman."

Ms. Glassman?

I'd been lying on my bed, so I sat up. "France, Mama?" How was I supposed to head off to France with Pops gone and Mama like that?

"And when you get back, it'll be just about time to get you to Iowa."

"I'll be fine here on my own," I told her. "Winter break starts in a few weeks. I can join you at Auntie's."

But she said, "I've put together a little money—for pocket change over there."

Seeing Mama like that, I remember thinking, Forget Iowa. Forget UT. There was Alamo Community College, right there in San Antonio. I could work construction and take classes at night, be close by to take care of Mama till she got right.

"For real," I told her. "I'll be fine here till I can come get youall in New Orleans."

And she lost it. "Dammit, Freeman!" Her neck was a twist of muscle, a vein popped at her temple. "I just can't worry after you right now."

Whenever we'd Skype after I came to France, she'd be smiling, and I'd smile, and I'd let her know that I was fine.

I'd say that we had beat the Ours or whoever, or that Georges and Françoise were real nice, and she'd always be like, "That's wonderful, Freeman. Have a good time."

Have a good time, she'd tell me.

But the thing is, I *was* having a good time. It felt like I shouldn't be.

I got back to the letter. I wadded it up and started from scratch on a new piece of paper. *Dear Mama*, I wrote. I told it like I would to Pops, like when I was walking around pretending he was with me and I was his tour guide, showing him the things I was learning about the city. I wrote all the details so she would see and smell and taste it. I told her about the roasted chestnuts they sold at Montmartre and how, from up there, you could look out over the entire city. I told her about Mont Blanc and fondue, about the classic A-frame chalets, the whole town smelling of woodsmoke. I told Mama how big my world was, and how I had her and Pops to thank for it.

To close, I wrote:

I know you don't like me to go on like this, but I need you to know that I know I'm not doing what I should. I'm not doing what Pops would do, if it was him in my shoes.

Youall are my family, my only family. I promise to never quit you like this again.

Love,

Me

MATT

The question my dad kept returning to was Why? Why did I leave Montreal without giving him a heads-up or an explanation? Each of the three days after his arrival, we'd walk the city and he'd pepper me with questions, but always, ultimately, it was back to that one question. I guess my answer was never quite satisfactory.

Maybe because I didn't quite know the answer myself. The divorce? Mom's new boyfriend? The pressure to go to Orford, to "succeed"?

Walking around the Friday night before his departure, he asked the question a little differently. "So tell me," he said, "what is it about Paris that you find so grand?"

I recited the words I'd been rehearsing since the night before, after reading an op-ed in *Libération*, a local newspaper.

"I read somewhere that Paris is a stage where we're all actors. Ever since I got here, I feel like I'm free to decide what role I want to play. For the first time in my life!"

He didn't respond but strode ahead.

White stone walk-ups lined the street. We were meeting Moose for dinner at L'Auberge Esclangon, a restaurant my dad had read about, over by Les Puces de Saint-Ouen, the famous flea market.

(Free and I had gone to the Puces one Sunday morning. After his shock at the mass of humanity and his fear that every other person was a pickpocket, he ended up negotiating for a boxful of battered *Astérix* comic books. He boasted about his "mad haggling skills," but to me, his purchase seemed a good deal only for the woman that had sold him the books. He paid 90 percent of the price that he could have had he bought them new at the FNAC bookstore, and got some that had been written in or were missing pages.)

"So tell me, Mathieu, what role is it you're playing on this...stage?"

"I don't know, Dad."

The street was quiet, even though we were only a few hundred yards away from the noisy, polluted ring road and the brassy shopping centers that ran along either side of it.

"Star quarterback," I said.

"You were that back home."

I *was*. That was the key word: *was*, past tense.

"Over here, I get to call my own plays," I said as a joke, to change the subject.

"It's great to be in a position to call your own shots," my dad said as we approached the restaurant, where Moose was waiting out front. "Coming here was the first of millions of decisions that will shape the rest of your life, that will determine the type of man you will become. So let me give you a piece of advice: Don't lie to yourself. The truth is a much better friend. You stole money. You ran away from your responsibilities. Face the man in the mirror.

"And by the way," he added, "I read the same article."

My dad looked genuinely pleased to see Moose again. He pulled him into a big hug. "I don't know if I should embrace you or put you over my knee for luring my son to run away from home."

Moose looked really happy to see my dad too. "I'd agree, I deserve the latter," he told him, "but I can't take credit for Matt's actions. You know that better than I do, Monsieur Dumas. Matt's his own man."

"You look great," my dad said to him. "Like a flamenco dancer."

In fact, Moose was way more dressed up than usual. With his hair slicked back, wearing dark cords, a cardinal-red shirt and black bomber jacket, he had the allure of a Spanish movie star.

Moose and my dad had gotten close in Montreal. Lots of French Under-20s players came every year for our training camps, but Moose was the only North African. My dad took him under his wing. He spent hours teaching Moose how to read defenses and run good, precise routes. Moose said it was my dad who made him realize that he wanted to be a teacher, helping kids from his neighborhood.

My dad asked him now, "So how's prep for graduation exams going?"

"The *bac*? So-so." Moose made a face. "My dad rides me about spending too much time on sports. He doesn't believe there's much of a future in it."

"Well, I'm not going to disagree. I tell Matt the same thing. There's more to life than sports." Before I could even say the thing about the pot and the kettle, he added, "Parents want better for their kids than they've had themselves."

Inside the restaurant, Moose stiffened when the maître d' greeted us. Moose never really seemed comfortable outside Villeneuve, which was probably why he rarely left it. He loosened again once we were alone at a table in the corner.

"It's too bad your friend Freeman couldn't join us," my dad said.

"He had a big dinner with his host family," I explained again. It was like my dad didn't remember what I'd already told him. "Georges, the father, invited some family friends to meet him. A government minister or something."

Moose looked surprised, though I'd assumed Free had told him too.

"What does his host father do?" my dad asked.

"A big businessman. For a telecom company, I think."

In fact, I knew he was an exec for the national telecom company, Orange S.A. I'm not sure why I was being so evasive. Maybe it was Moose's smirk, like this information confirmed something he'd always suspected about Freeman.

"Still, I'd have liked to meet him," my dad said.

He sounded as suspicious as Juliette originally had been, as judgmental as Moose now looked.

"Freeman is a good player," Moose said. "He's also *very* American and a bit moody."

"Look who's talking, Mister Personal-Foul-Who-Blows-Up-at-the-Ref-Every-Other-Play," I said.

"I'm not moody," Moose said. "I'm spirited."

My dad interrupted. "What do you mean, *very American*?"

"You know," Moose said. "He's kind of what you'd expect. His father is in the army in Iraq, and he believes America is the world's savior and that all Muslims want to fly planes into American skyscrapers."

"What?" I said. "He doesn't think that"—even though Free kind of did—"not any more than you consider all Americans oil-thirsty capitalists."

"Aren't they?"

"That's like me saying that all North Africans think the same. Like me calling you Moroccan when you're Algerian."

"As a matter of fact, I'm French," Moose said.

"Are you two finished?" said my father, putting on his reading glasses and passing around the menus the maître d' had left in a stack on the table.

We read them in silence. I didn't know why I was defending Freeman so aggressively. I guess I didn't want my dad to disapprove of my friendship with him, even though he'd probably never meet him.

After the waiter took our orders, my dad asked Moose, "Do you plan on coming back next summer?"

"To Montreal? I'd love to, but I still have to reimburse the Diables Rouges the money they lent me for last summer's trip."

"Just know that you're always welcome to stay at my house," my dad said. "I have a spare bedroom."

Then he added, "To pay off your debts is very important. Staying free of debt, that's the only way to be truly free, free from the control of others."

And I couldn't help it: I laughed.

"Someone trying to send a message?" I said.

"You'd do well to take heed of it, *petit gars*! The world's not just fun and games, and it sure as hell doesn't revolve only around you."

I was as surprised as Moose seemed to be by the outburst. I stared off into the room.

The rest of the meal went like that, me mostly silent, Moose and Dad seeming to have a pleasant enough time without me.

» » » »

When I showed up at his hotel the next morning to accompany him to the airport, my father was already standing outside, the old backpack he'd had since his traveling days in the '80s at his feet. I was carrying my gear bag with me; I wouldn't have time to go back to the apartment before our game that afternoon. We walked toward the Arc de Triomphe to catch the RER.

"What about those Anges Bleus?" my dad asked. "Are they any good?"

I knew he was genuinely curious, but by his tone of voice I could tell he was also trying to make up for his outburst at dinner in front of Moose.

"They're ranked two higher than us. And they're big—Gold's Gym types. One-on-one, any one of them can pancake any of our guys."

"So what's your plan?"

"They have this QB from Ottawa, likes to fling the ball around."

"Anyone I've heard of?" he asked.

"Alain Laplante or Lamarque—I don't remember."

He paid for our tickets at the kiosk in the RER station and shook his head, not recognizing the name. We walked toward the platform.

"They always start him in the first half," I said. "Try to run up the score. To protect their lead, they hand the ball off to their star running back in the second."

The train arrived, and we boarded.

"So what will you do, then?" my dad asked.

"Mix it up. The coaches and Free and I came up with the idea to shut down the pass in the first half. We'll line up in our nickel and dime packages on defense and give them the run. Then I come out slinging in the second half, when their Canadian QB's on the sideline and they can't play catch-up."

"That's one stone-cold bluff," he said.

"It's a stone-cold world," I said, sounding like Freeman.

"I wish you luck."

We were switching trains at Les Halles station, from the A to the B line, struggling with our bags in the rushing mass of people.

"Don't we make our own luck?" I said. "Isn't that what you always taught me?"

He didn't say anything, just pushed forward through the crowd.

We were sitting side by side on the train. My dad still hadn't responded. Finally he said, "Promise me, Mathieu, that you'll never run away again."

He stared at me until I met his gaze.

"It's okay to run *after* things, but not *away* from them. They always catch up to you."

We sat in silence. The train we were on, an airport express, zoomed by Villeneuve-La-Grande but didn't stop.

I pointed to the Cinq Mille projects. "That's where Moose lives. Our field is right behind those buildings."

"Now I understand why you prefer to live at Juliette's. It looks like East Berlin before the fall of the Wall."

You start to forget after a while, I thought. The bleakness just becomes normal.

I pointed to the parabolic antennas riveted to what seemed like every other window. "At least they all have satellite TV."

"Great. They can watch Al Jazeera."

"You sounded like Mom just then," I told him.

My dad laughed. "I did, didn't I?"

I had to leave him at airport security. We stood there. I tried to act like I wasn't choked up. Dad wasn't even trying.

An old Air France 747 rolled by the giant plate-glass windows, on the other side of the metal detectors and X-ray scanners. I told him, "Between what I've gotten from the team and what I took, I still have about $450, tucked away at Juliette's. I could send it to Mom as a sign of good faith."

He rolled his eyes. "It's a little late for good faith."

He removed his wallet from his back pocket and handed me one of his credit cards.

"In case of emergencies," he said. "But *only* in case of emergencies."

We hugged each other a long time before he finally let me go.

ANGES BLEUS (2–1) V. DIABLES ROUGES (2–1)
MARCH 14

MATT

At halftime, the score was 24–14 for the Anges Bleus.

"The greatest game plan in the world don't mean squat when you're losing by ten," Free said as we exited the locker rooms at the Beach.

He was only half right. We were still in the game, so our plan was on track. Only now I had to produce the two scores we were down by, and I was a little banged up.

I had played safety in the first half, the fifth back in our nickel scheme, and on one third-down play I took on their running back, "Choo-Choo," who had a good thirty pounds on me, all muscle. I stopped him, but he about broke me in two. Now I could barely turn my head to the left.

The stands were more empty than not. It was a cold, wet day. The Anges Bleus kicked the ball off to open the third quarter. They'd learned their lesson in the first half and kicked it away from Free, high but not too deep. Sidi fielded the ball—and got hammered the instant he touched it. The scattered crowd went "Oomph!" as he got hit, then started to roar, cheering, even though it was our own guy getting clobbered. I could see the hoodie boys by the oak pumping their fists in the air.

"*Allez*, Sidi! Get up!" I heard over the crowd. "Show them you can take whatever they dish out!"

It was Aïda, in a red-and-white headscarf—the team colors—standing down the sideline a little ways. Sidi wobbled back to the bench.

"And that goes for you too, *mec*," she growled at me as I passed, jogging out to our forming huddle. "Get it going!"

The Anges Bleus knew I was a little shaken up, so they came after me extra hard on each play. Still, I got us back in it on our first drive, hitting our tight end, a French kid named Jean-Marc, on two straight passes, then lofting a long one to Moose on a skinny post.

Anges Bleus 24–Diables Rouges 21.

Our defense forced them to punt on the next drive. Free brought it back to their forty, the punter pushing him out of bounds on our sidelines.

He flipped me the ball as he passed where I was standing. "Now go get 'em," he told me.

And I did. We did.

The Anges Bleus kept putting eight men in the box, blitzing off the corner, trying to get to me. Our O-line did a great job, and I picked them apart. Five passes to Moose on five different routes: a hitch, a curl, a slant, a drag, a quick out. Mobylette ran it in from eight yards out.

Anges Bleus 24–Diables Rouges 28.

Their Canadian quarterback was on the bench, screaming at their offense to bury us. But we put eight men in the box too, with Free at middle linebacker so he could roam. He was too quick for their lineman to get to, and he took on Choo-Choo on every play. They tried a pass to change it up, and our defensive end, Chorizo (his real name was Felipe), came off the corner and stripped the Anges Bleus' French QB, scooped up the ball and ran it in.

Anges Bleus 24–Diables Rouges 35.

It went on like that, Free and the D blowing up their offense, me picking apart their defense. Sidi was a little off after getting tagged on the opening kick; I kept throwing at him, and he dropped every ball. But Moose and Mobylette, everyone else, had a field day. Flag routes, stops-and-goes, even a flea flicker. We won 49–27.

Almost the entire team, forty guys or so, goofed off in the locker room afterward, boasting about big hits they'd made, singing group songs, laughing. Their retelling of the game went like this: all looked lost, and when Sidi got steam-rollered to open the second half, everyone expected more of the same. ("The line didn't block for me!" Sidi protested. "Go screw yourselves!" And he stormed into the showers.) Then we turned it around the very next drive, the story continued. Like Drew Brees and the Saints in the Super Bowl. Like champions.

Outside in the parking lot, Aïda and Yasmina waited for us. Yasmina's headscarf was team-colored too.

"You should've seen the faces of the Anges Bleus when they boarded their bus." Aïda couldn't speak a word without her fingers dancing on the air, restating her sentences in this other odd language. "They looked shell-shocked, like they couldn't believe they'd lost to the lowly Diables Rouges." And she laughed.

Others made their way over. Moose, Mobylette and the rest retold—yet again—the story of how David slew the mighty Goliath, one talking over the other. Even Sidi joined in.

Listening to them, I realized how much these guys were what my dad called "born underdogs." It was like their daily lives were driven by one lone notion: to just get by, in the rough *cités*, at their sorry ghetto school, even in their huge families. But as much as fighting to get by was in their blood, the idea of prevailing, of coming out on top, wasn't. It was like our victory had stunned them even more than it had the Anges Bleus. All the pre-game bluster aside, the Diables Rouges would probably have been just as happy playing the Anges Bleus tough and losing in a squeaker. Deep inside, it was likely what they had expected would happen.

"Coach Thierry says the Caïmans, next week, are a much better team," Free said to quiet things down. "Probably second only to the Jets."

(His French had really gotten quite good.)

"They are," Moose said. "They beat the Jets last year in the final and are undefeated so far this season."

"So far..." Free said, and he grinned.

Guys started to wander off. It was just us four—Freeman and me, Moose and Sidi. And the two girls, of course.

"So, what now?" Free asked, and I said, "Why don't we go down to Paris?"

Sidi and Moose looked at each other, visibly not so hot on the idea.

"Paris?" said Sidi.

"Sure," I said. "Let's go to the Champs-Élysées. It's what the French do to celebrate, right?"

Aïda jumped in. "Please take us with you."

Our tackle, Claude Benayoun, emerged from the locker room and asked what we were up to. I looked at Sidi, who was looking at Moose, who was looking toward Aïda and Yasmina.

"Papa'll kill me if he finds out," Sidi said.

"How will he find out?" Aïda shot back.

"What about the cops?" Moose said. "They aren't too keen about guys from this zip code wandering around down there."

Free laughed. "If it's cops that are the problem, we're more likely to get a rough time here in Villeneuve."

I looked at my cell phone. "It's not even dinnertime yet; it's still early. We can play baby-foot at the Chicago Pizza Pie Factory."

I knew how much Moose and Sidi loved foosball.

But Moose still looked reluctant. "I was already down there once this week, with your father," he said. "That's plenty for me."

"Unless you guys are afraid to go into the big city, that is," I added.

"Yeah right," Moose said, but it didn't mean, *Okay, let's go*. He stood there frozen, Sidi beside him, and Claude beside them, looking silently on.

"We'll just hang out," Aïda said, her tone defiant, challenging them. "Only for a couple of hours."

Being called out by a girl was the determining factor.

Sidi said, "Let's go."

MATT

Sidi lit a joint the second we came up from underground. We were clustered in a group under the Arc de Triomphe, a stone's throw from the Tomb of the Unknown Soldier. The two girls tossed a football back and forth, underhanded, on the gray stone pavement. The tomb was just a roped-off grave, a small flame burning at its head.

Free shook his head when Claude extended the spleef to him, and Moose waved it off too. "You know I don't do that," he said. "American football is my drug."

I took the joint. "I love football too. But hey, it's a celebration." I sucked deep, deep, deep and tried to keep the smoke in, down in my lungs.

I burst into a fit of coughing.

The others, smokers and not, were laughing like crazy, but I had to sit on the ground. I rested against one of the Arc's four pillars to catch my breath and stared out at the horde of cars fighting their way around the chaotic roundabout. Place de l'Étoile: twelve avenues channeling toward the Arc de Triomphe. I'd seen a postcard of it, shot at night from above, and the intersection looked like a brightly lit star. (Or a giant asterisk, really.)

I looked over at Freeman joshing with Aïda and Yasmina—he snatched the ball from Aïda's hands and she snatched it back just as quickly—and I realized they both had the same quicksilver temperaments. Over to one side was Moose, kicking up into a handstand. "Wazzup," he said, walking by me upside down. I didn't know where Sidi and Claude had disappeared to.

The next thing I knew, Moose went crashing down onto his head. I started laughing like a maniac, but Moose lay on his back, motionless. I jumped up then, and we all ran over to him. Sidi and Claude had come back too. (I couldn't help it, I was still giggling from the weed.)

"Don't touch him," Aïda ordered.

I thought he was out cold, until his chest started bouncing and he was hiccupping spits of laughter.

Sidi and I helped him sit up. He rubbed the top of his head with both hands. "That hurt," he said.

Sidi shot the bird and waved it back and forth in front of Moose's face. "How many fingers do you see?"

Free said, "Let's go to the Pizza Pie Factory."

Everyone but Aïda and me took off running into the street, zigzagging through the lock of traffic around l'Étoile. Cars honked, drivers yelled the usual French insults: "*Connards*!" "*Enculés*!"—Assholes! Fuckers! She and I took the pedestrian tunnel that passed underneath l'Etoile to the Champs-Élysées.

"So what do you do with all your free time?" Aïda asked. She was carrying the football. "I mean, when you're not playing or coaching."

The tunnel was well lit but empty. Classical music played from speakers that I looked for but couldn't see.

"Free and I go to movies. Sometimes we visit museums, or people-watch at the Jardins du Luxembourg or at the Tuileries."

We were speaking French, only French. It felt good. With Freeman, even when we were speaking French, I tended to think in English because with him we shifted back and forth so much.

"Sometimes, if we don't have practice," I told her, "there's a bar in Les Halles where we hang out."

(Well, twice we'd hung out there, and we'd only ordered sodas.)

Aïda tossed me the ball. "You and Freeman are like a married couple."

"Ha! Right."

I jogged ahead a little and tossed the ball behind my back to her. She caught it naturally, with her hands.

"No, Free and I mostly walk around and try to get to know the greatest city on Earth."

She put the ball in her backpack, did that thing with her mouth like Freeman sometimes did. "*Tsst.* You say that because you only know postcard Paris."

"I play football in Villeneuve, remember?"

"But you don't live there."

"And you're in a position to judge?" I said. "Your father doesn't even let you spend time down here in the city."

She didn't respond immediately. "I know more than you think I do, Mathieu Dumas," she said finally.

The honking from the street above faded in then. I'd forgotten where we were.

"Do you read?" she said.

"Books?"

She laughed. "What else is there to read?"

"I read *Libération* every day, on the metro or having my *café du matin*," I said. "And lots of magazines too."

"No books though?"

I felt kind of small all of a sudden. "Not as much as I should."

"I have one I think you'll like. I'll bring it to practice Monday."

We were walking side by side.

"You're seventeen?" I said.

"Same as you."

I hesitated, not knowing how to ask my question. So I just said it. "Who makes you wear the headscarf?"

"Why, Al-Qaida, of course." She started to laugh. "Stupid."

"It's not funny—I just don't know."

"You know why I wear the hijab?" she said. "Because I can. Because it's part of my heritage."

"No one forces you?"

"Do I seem like the submissive type?"

We were nearing the exit.

"Nobody compels me to wear it. Not my father, not my Imam. The French government tells me I can't wear it at school, which makes me want to wear it everywhere else all the more."

She removed it, a wave of brown hair spilling over her shoulders. I felt kind of uncomfortable seeing her like that. It was almost like she'd taken off her shirt or something.

"Aïda!" We heard Sidi's voice from just outside the tunnel.

She backed away from me, gathering her hair up in the white-and-red cloth.

"What's going on?" Sidi said, halfway down the stairs.

Aïda didn't answer. I stayed silent too.

He was glaring at her. "The others are waiting," he said.

We walked in an awkward silence, Sidi between us. All the same, I got stuck on the image of Aïda with her hair down.

Moose, Free, Claude and Yasmina sat crammed together on a public bench outside the tunnel. The sidewalk was noisy and chaotic, filled with people speaking many different languages.

"All right," I said, "foosball time!"

"Sidi and I are going to whoop your North American butts," Moose boasted, popping up off the bench and striding down the Champs-Élysées.

"Bring it," Free shot back. But then he whispered to me in English, "You best be good, 'cause I ain't hardly ever played before."

Free and I had been to the Pizza Pie Factory three or four times, each time more lively than the one before. It was the closest thing to a genuine American sports joint in Paris: spunky waitresses (mostly Brits and Irish, by their accents), so-so pizzas but good burgers, and buffalo wings (the sauce tasted like ketchup and Tabasco, but it was better than nothing). There were TVs in every corner that looped reruns of NFL games nonstop, and a game room with pool and foosball tables. One time we went, each of us ordered a beer, and they served us.

It was Saturday night, so there was a lineup to get in, twenty people or so standing alongside the plate-glass window with the pink '55 Chevy in it. Three bouncers—a North African and two black guys—each with a neck as thick as my thigh, monitored the front door, letting one or two people pass, then blocking the entrance. Freeman was chatting up two preppy girls in front of us. Aïda and Yasmina stood together, kind of sheepish, whispering. Sidi was still brooding, off to the side. "They're not going to let us in," he said.

"Why wouldn't they?" I said. "Free and I come here all the time."

Sidi turned and faced the traffic on the Champs.

One of the bouncers signaled the girls talking to Freeman. Free tagged behind them, and I followed him. As I passed through the entrance, I heard one of the bouncers saying, "Sorry, private party." The guy draped his huge arm across the doorway. Moose and the others stood on the other side.

"We're with them," Moose said. He pointed to Freeman and me, standing beside the pink Chevy.

"*Désolé*," the North African bouncer said. "You can't go in."

"But why us and not them?" I asked.

"We're all together," Yasmina said just outside the door.

The bouncers didn't seem open to negotiation. One kept his arm across the doorway, and another repeated, "Private party."

"We heard you the first time," Sidi jumped in, jabbing his finger at the guy.

Moose turned to hold Sidi back. "Calm down," he said, but Sidi was screaming, "Answer the question, asshole. Why them and not us?"

Claude was standing next to Sidi now, and he rivaled the bouncers for size. The people behind them, preppy kids and American wannabes, started shifting around, some talking under their breath.

"Why them and not us?" Aïda repeated, her eyes as fiery hot as her brother's. "I'll tell you. Because he's *cistera*!"—Racist.

The North African bouncer shot her a knowing smile. More of a leer. "*Allez, dégagez maintenant.*"

He had the same accent as Aïda and Sidi, as Moose, the same you-messing-with-me look as the hoodie boys. He could be from Villeneuve, just like them, for all we knew.

"Forget y'all," Freeman snapped, pushing past the bouncers and back outside.

I was right behind him. "Yeah, forget y'all," I said in English too.

We swaggered off down the Champs-Élysées, laughing like we didn't care about getting in, Sidi a few feet back, pointing back at the *Beur* bouncer. "We're going to be out here when you get off!" he threatened. "We'll be waiting for you!"

Aïda and Yasmina finally dragged him away.

When we were down the street from the club, Moose wheeled into me. "Didn't we tell you, Matt!" He was red-faced and fuming, the way he'd been with Juliette's concierge the day I arrived.

"Tell me what?" I said.

"That they wouldn't let a bunch of *Beurs* into your club."

My club?

"But he was *Beur* too," I said. "That wasn't about racism. He let Freeman in."

"It wasn't?" Moose said. "What was it about then?"

"The guy was an asshole, that's all."

Sidi hawked and spat on the ground. He got out some papers to roll another joint. People around didn't seem to notice. Moose stared past me.

Aïda said, "It *is* about racism, Mathieu, but it goes beyond just skin color. It's as much about where we come from and what we wear as skin color."

"I don't get it," I said.

They all burst out laughing. Freeman too.

"You are *so* white," Moose said.

I decided to laugh along with them. Not because I agreed, but because they were my friends and I didn't want to be left out.

FREE

Matt looked all stunned when Moose called him white, even more than he had when Moose and them got shut out of the Pizza Pie Factory. Nobody was really talking anymore. There was a McDonald's a few doors up the way, so I said, "Royals with cheese, anyone?"

Sidi fired up his doobie, like he didn't care who was watching. "I gotta finish my smoke."

The rest of us went on in. Except Matt. He sat with Sidi on a green wooden bench.

McDonald's restaurants in Paris are swankier than back home, more McBistro than McSupersize Me. Moose, Claude, Yasmina and me stood in line; Aïda went off to the bathroom. A ten-foot plastic Ronald looked down at us, his face a lot warmer than those of the two security guards standing by the cash registers. An Arab and a Brother, like at the Pizza Pie. They eyeballed us the whole time we were ordering. We took our grub to a bank of tables off to the side and sat next to three girls eating strawberry sundaes. Hotties. Brunettes, very French.

Through the glass, I watched Sidi extend the doobie toward Matt. Matt shook his head but said something to him; he looked like Moose does when he's jawing at me about something I already know. Sidi didn't respond, kind of ignoring him, looking off down the avenue. Then he hit the doobie hard and flicked away the roach. He got up and came inside. Matt followed. The security guards hawked them as they walked to where we were sitting.

Matt could be naïve, it was true. Like outside the Pizza Pie. Or with the riot cops up in Villeneuve. He couldn't see that the cops weren't interested in him, only in me and Moose, that they were leaving him be.

But he made a good point too—like right then. It wasn't Sidi being North African, having the wrong zip code and whatnot, that had caught the attention of those two guards. It was that he was camped outside their glass doors smoking a doobie, straight up out in the open, for everyone to see.

Come on now. For real? How were they *not* going to be sizing him up?

Sidi sat next to Aïda, closest to the French girls.

"Want something?" Matt asked him.

Sidi pulled some coins out of his jeans pocket, tossed them onto the tabletop. "Bring me a strawberry sundae," he said, kind of dismissive, and Matt moved off.

Sidi smiled a sleazy smile at the French girls. "They really *do* look good." He was eyeballing the girls and not their ice cream. "Are they as good as they look?"

The girls ignored him, Aïda slugged his arm, but he still leered.

"Eh! I'm talking to you," he said.

"No you're not," one of the girls shot back. "You're slurring at us."

I couldn't tell who laughed first, the girls or me, but it was my arm that Aïda clutched. "Don't get him started," she whispered.

But it was too late. Sidi moved to a chair at the girls' table. "You too good to talk to me?"

He grabbed the sundae of the one who had cracked on him and put a spoonful into his mouth.

"Give it back!" the girl said.

"You don't look so superior now," he said, his mouth full of pink and white ice cream.

"What's your problem, *espèce de grosse merde*"—You piece of shit.

"Takes one to know one, and I can tell by looking at that tight bourgeois ass of yours that you're a dirty little piece."

Matt was off at the register, ordering. Moose and Aïda and Yasmina just looked on. Claude was picking at his food like nothing was happening.

The French girls gathered their stuff to leave, but Sidi pushed in close to the sassy one, blocking her in, his face only inches from hers. "We should go for a walk, just you and me."

"Fuck off," the girl said, now flushed and about to cry.

"Enough!" I said and reached over and grabbed Sidi by the sleeve.

He snapped it free.

"Come on, Sidi," I heard Matt say, suddenly there beside us. The lady at the register called after him, saying he had left behind his order.

The three girls, ghost white, scooted off up the aisle and out the door.

"Stop making an ass of yourself," Matt said.

Sidi turned from me and got all up in Matt's face.

Moose and Aïda, Yasmina and Claude, they just looked on.

"Me? Making an ass of myself?" Sidi's voice quavered. "Bitches talk down to me and you get their backs instead of mine?"

"You gave them all the reasons in the world to treat you like shit," Matt said, all calm.

Sidi shook his head from side to side, disappointed-like. Then he grabbed Matt by the collar and drove him back into the wall!

"You think you can just come here, all *grand seigneur*, and tell us how to live?"

Matt's a head taller, but Sidi has probably been in a jillion more fights. Matt, his collar bunched in Sidi's fist, said, "Let go of me," his voice still calm.

"You need to let him go," I said—in English, to make my point.

Moose was there too then, but he was fronting up on me. On me! Like he was about to throw down.

Aïda, she was looking at her feet. Yasmina and Claude too.

"*Qu'est-ce qui se passe, là?*"—What's going on here?

"Let's go! Out, out!"

It was the security guards, both barking. One had Sidi by the scruff of the neck, the other had Matt, and we were all being ushered toward, then shoved through, the front doors. On the sidewalk, in the mass of moving people, we all gathered ourselves. But we were clearly of two camps: Matt and me, and the rest.

Matt stared at Moose, looking all puppy-dog hurt. "Moose?"

Moose smirked, then turned to the others. "You know how it is with *les blancs*"—with white boys—he said, like it meant me too. "Sometimes you just have to put them in their place."

He started walking away. The others followed. Aïda glanced back at us as she left.

"Fuck you, Moose!" Matt shouted. "No wonder they call you *racailles*! If you act like scum, people treat you like scum!"

I grabbed him, held him back from following them, all the tourists on the avenue staring. "Come on, Matt," I said. "It ain't nothing."

He pulled free of my hold. We watched them saunter off toward the RER. Sidi shot us the bird over his shoulder.

"Fuck this shithole," Matt said and walked off in the other direction.

CAÏMANS (3–1) V. DIABLES ROUGES (3–1)
MARCH 29

FREE

"Come on, Free," Matt kept saying, "it'll be fun."

It was the Friday after the dustup on the Champs, and me and Matt were on the RER, headed back to Paris after the last practice before our game against the Caïmans on Sunday. The Caïmans were ranked right behind the Jets, but it wasn't the importance of the game that made me be like, *Tsst.* Hitchhike to Normandy? I was thinking. People got killed hitchhiking. Or kidnapped or who knew what.

But he insisted. "An adventure..."

Like him and me needed more adventure.

"What about all that 'you act like you're on vacation' stuff you was snapping at me about at practice?" I said.

"Well, when we aren't at practice or a game, we *are* on vacation."

I stayed silent, staring straight ahead.

Practices had been terrible all week. Scattershot attendance, guys acting cold to me and Matt, Moose and Sidi avoiding us altogether. At flag-team practice, Aïda and Yasmina weren't particularly warm either. I knew it was because of the madness at the McDonald's, but still and all, two wins from qualifying for the Under-20s title seemed like a bad time to go blasé-blah on the season.

At that last practice, there hadn't even been enough folks to field two full sides—seventeen, maybe eighteen total, and a lot of those present were some real scrubs. Coach Thierry ran us instead, more wind sprints than I'd ever done in one session: ten 20-yard dashes, then ten 30-yard dashes, then ten 40-yarders, then back down the ladder, hardly any time to recover in between. Like us who had turned up were to blame for the others not being there.

So I asked, "Have you even hitchhiked before?"

He didn't answer. Instead he said, "Listen, it'll be Saturday morning, so lots of traffic headed toward the coast."

"Can we even make it there and back in one day?"

"It's two hundred kilometers—like, a two-hour drive each way. We'll be home in time for supper."

I looked out the train window, even though there was nothing to see but dark tunnel.

"It feels like spring already," he said. "Beautiful days."

"And still freezing at night."

He was all excitable. "Free," he said.

"Tsst."

"Freeee..."

Hitchhiking. For real?

At eight the next morning I walked the few blocks to Charles de Gaulle–Étoile RER station. Matt was already on the platform waiting for me when I arrived.

"It's on like *Donkey Kong*," he said, still all excitable.

He'd made this sign, a rectangle of cardboard with *NORMANDIE/LES PLAGES* written in thick black marker. He'd told Juliette, like I'd told Georges and Françoise, about the day trip, just not about the mode of transportation. We let them assume we were taking the train. "*This trip will be very educational*," Georges had said. "*You do very well to take this initiative*."

I was wearing my letter jacket over a jean jacket. I'd even put on a knit cap. "It's nippy as all get-out," I said to Matt.

"Buck up, laddie!" he said in this hokey Brit accent.

It wasn't funny.

We took the red line to the end, Poissy. The entrance to the highway was three or four kilometers away, apparently, and Matt figured out which bus would get us closest. I let him do the work. The number 51 dropped us at this huge hospital complex, and a security guard pointed us in the right direction. We walked up the sidewalk, Matt's pace determined. He led me to the A13 highway, a steady buzz of cars zipping by even at nine fifteen on a Saturday morning.

"We're not supposed to actually go onto the highway, I guess," Matt said. "The cops will run us off."

"How will we get a ride then?"

"We'll stand here." He stopped at the base of the on-ramp. "Lose the tuque," he said. "Makes you look thuggish."

I did as I was told. Matt, beaming this huge smile, faced the oncoming traffic, one foot on the embankment, the other nearly in the road, holding the *NORMANDIE/ LES PLAGES* sign way out. And just like that, a brown Peugeot swerved over onto the shoulder and stopped a few yards past where we were standing.

And I was like, *For real?*

Matt jogged to the passenger door, which the driver had pushed open, and leaned in. "We're headed to Caen," he said.

The driver, a darker-looking guy, maybe North African, said, "You are fortunate." He didn't smile, and his French was heavily accented and choppy. "I can take you."

Matt climbed in back, which left me to sit in the front seat beside the dude. He pulled out into the traffic, and we headed for the coast. Not even two minutes on the side of the road. Just like that.

He drove really fast but didn't say anything. He wore a suit coat and shirt but no tie and had a head of thick graying black hair, high on top like a pompadour, and a thick black mustache. Wired eyes aside, he kind of looked like that old-guy actor Burt Reynolds.

From the back, Matt introduced himself.

I said, "My name is Freeman. *Bonjour*."

"You are American?" Burt Reynolds said.

"Canadian," Matt said, but Burt Reynolds had been talking to me.

I said, "*Oui*."

He didn't say anything more, just faced forward, eyes wired.

Before long we were out of the city, driving through the countryside and flying, pedal to the metal. I tried to give Matt a discreet *What's up with this dude?* look, but he ignored me. He asked the driver, "Do you live in Caen?"

"Cherbourg," Burt Reynolds said, "an hour beyond. I work at port."

It was silent again.

"We're students," Matt said from the back, a straight-up lie. "Study abroad in Paris."

Burt Reynolds didn't seem to care. He focused on the road.

"We're going to visit the D-day beaches," Matt said. "Not for school or anything. Just because we're curious. 'Know your history or repeat it,' you know. That sort of thing."

Burt Reynolds didn't care.

When Matt said, "We're also semiprofessional footballers," the dude perked up. He looked over at me, his crazy eyes asking, *But you are American?*

"*Le football américain*," I explained.

"They play here?"

"Our team is the Diables Rouges of Villeneuve," Matt said.

"Villeneuve," he said. "I have cousins who live there."

He looked over at me, then forward again. "Yes, I think I have seen posters of your American football."

Matt said, "Are you coming from Villeneuve this morning?"

"No," he said. "From Turkey."

"Turkey?"

"Thirty-seven hours on road," he said. "Well, thirty-eight, with the stop in Strasbourg."

"Do you have family in Strasbourg?" Matt asked.

"My wife. I drove from my family home in Turkey to kill her."

Neither Matt nor I said anything.

Turkish Burt Reynolds, telling his story in thick English now (for my benefit, I imagined), explained that before taking the job at the port in Normandy, he'd been a long-haul trucker for a company based out of Strasbourg, in eastern France, and he had married a French woman there. He commuted between Cherbourg and Strasbourg on weekends, and when he could, he would book it back to his family home in Turkey. (It was a complicated story to follow.) He said that he had been in Turkey with his mother, father and brothers in a village called Nagdy or Nigdy or some such (I couldn't make out the word), and he *knew*—"I just knowing," he said—that his wife was cheating on him.

"I jump into car on spot"—he snapped his fingers with a *pop!*—"and drive back to France to cut her throat."

"Of course you did," Matt said from the back.

"When I arrive she is gone, with my son and all my valuables." He threw his hands into the air. "The apartment, empty." Burt Reynolds looked genuinely hurt, but about her or the empty apartment was unclear.

"Now I must return to work at port or lose my job," he said. "Without port, I would have to drive truck again. This is no life."

"Not any life I can imagine," Matt said from the back.

» » » »

Turkish Burt Reynolds turned out to be a real Chatty Cathy once he got going. He jawed at us the whole way, steady, in English. It was like talking helped him keep his mind off having failed to kill his wife. He told us about Caen and the Normandy beaches and everything. Really useful stuff, actually. As a former trucker, he knew all about the region.

He dropped us in the town center, way out of his way, just past noon. "You must remember to visit memorial museum," he said. "The Museum of Peace, it is called. Also buses there, take you to beaches."

We waved like mad as he pulled away. His car turned the corner and I was like, "Matt, man, a killer just spent mad energy counseling us to visit the Museum of Peace. *Peace*, man."

We were both bent over double, laughing.

"Hitchhiking is fun!" I said.

"Yeah, it is," he agreed.

Matt tossed out knuckles, and I bumped my fist against his.

The sun was high overhead, and the sky ocean blue, a cool wind breezing. It must have been pushing seventy degrees. I took off my letter jacket.

Matt said, "Let's find some lunch."

There was a crepe stand on the corner. I ordered ham and cheese. The lady behind the round flat grill fried an egg and put it over the ham and sprinkled grated Gruyère over it all; it was so good that after one bite I ordered another.

"Ah, the Americans are hungry today," she said in English.

"Very hungry," I said.

"Hungry for experience," said Matt, looking all proud at his wit. He added in French, "And I'm *Québecois*, by the way."

Me and Matt did that a lot—switching from French to English, back and forth, like they were both just one language. It was funny how speaking French so much had gotten me speaking English better too—understanding things about grammar I'd never thought on before, using more varied vocabulary. Mama would get a kick out of that.

We sat on a city bench to eat our crepes, and Matt, suddenly all serious, said, "Do you think I should apologize to Moose and Sidi?"

"For what?"

He looked off up the street. "For bad-mouthing them."

"Sidi had you by the neck!"

"But I treated them like white people always treat them."

I wanted to say, *But Matt, you* are *white*...

I didn't. It would have been mean. And it didn't feel quite right either. I just focused my attention on my crepe.

"Okay, maybe not Sidi," Matt said. "He was acting like an ass. But Moose is my friend."

He wasn't your friend that night, I thought, but I didn't say that either.

"I said something stupid, okay?" Matt said. "Still, that doesn't explain what's going on with the team."

"Sure it does," I said between bites. "They're acting all Three Musketeers. 'One for all, and all for one.' You mess with one of them, all of them get mad behind it."

"No, it feels like something else. Like the guys are afraid all of a sudden."

"Afraid? Of what? We're killing folks."

"My dad always tells his players that being a middle-of-the-pack team is easy," Matt said. "Being on top, that's a totally different pressure."

He finished his crepe, wadded the paper and leaned back, all stretched out on the bench.

"Fear of failure," he said. "It's like they're paralyzed by the idea of coming up short against the Caïmans. Like, if they don't show up to practice, if they act like they don't care and don't give it one hundred percent, then they don't have to step up. If we lose, they can pretend it was because they weren't really invested in winning in the first place."

"Fear of failure?" I said. "Or of success maybe."

I wadded up my empty crepe wrappers and wiped my greasy lips.

"My sophomore year, we were playing John Jay High," I said. "The Mustangs—huge rivals. It was our homecoming, and they were ranked at the top of our district, number two in Texas 5-A, had a couple of All-Staters on defense. I was *on* though. I was playing running back, and in our first offensive series we drove the length of the field on two of my runs, a thirty- and a fifty-yarder. We had the ball first and goal on the seven, and Coach Calley called an inside dive to me. I popped through a quick hole, past the linebacker. Number 56. He grunted, *Shit!* as I blew by. Nobody left but the free safety, and I juked him, cut hard against the flow."

Suddenly I heard my own voice, the words spilling out.

"He punched the ball loose. Like he wasn't even going for the tackle."

I heard my voice, and my words surprised me, because they sounded like a confession.

"They recovered."

Matt said, "It's funny how the bad memories are the ones that stick with you."

"The weird thing was that he knew. The free safety, I mean."

Matt looked like he didn't quite follow.

"Our stadium manager called me into their locker room after the game, after they'd showered and left. All over—on the floors, under benches and taped to lockers—was my head shot from the program, taped to note cards with my tendencies written on the back. *An outside runner; quick; a fumbler; carries the ball with only one hand, even on the goal line.*

"I wasn't number 17, just a helmet and pads playing running back. I had a face. They knew my face."

"That's cool. Or, at least, flattering," Matt said. "Did you win?"

"Nope. I didn't have another run longer than five yards after that first drive."

"Why not?"

"Who knows," I said. "Fear of failure."

"Or of success?"

"Maybe. Coach Calley moved me to corner the next game; he said my future was playing on defense. I guess that's why he's the coach and I ain't nothing but a player. He sees things I don't really see.

"So where to?" I asked, rising—and changing the subject.

"Why, the Museum of Peace, of course."

FREE

The ticket to the museum was *really* expensive—80 Euros, like, $125, the student rate!—more than I'd budgeted for the entire week. At least it included a minibus tour of the beaches. And the museum was worth it, way impressive. They showed these films about D-day—nothing you didn't already know from school and all the movies, but it was something else to see for real. And there were tons of photos and memorabilia, the uniforms of all the units and stuff, their weapons—straight-up relics.

I bought some postcards from the gift shop. Mama and I had taken to writing each other, paper and pencil, after that first letter. I'd been sending three, sometimes four, a week. I wrote at night, before going to bed, and I would tell her about what I'd done that day, places Matt and me had visited, things I'd learned about Paris or France or the world. Hers were scribbles on scrap paper mostly, sometimes hardly more than *I'm fine* and *Have fun*. I mean, she's got so much to do, and Tookie and Tina to worry after too. Tookie would usually write a few words at the bottom in those big block letters you first learn, and Tina sent crayon drawings she'd made for me.

I would carry Mama's letters with me, unopened, in my jacket pocket until the next one arrived, sometimes days and days on end. Because once I'd read it, it was like the letter was suddenly just ink on a page, you know, and I would lose sight of them, of Mama and Tookie and Tina. The weight of it in my pocket, the anticipation of the still-unseen words, made Mama and them seem real and right here with me. Like the next line in a conversation that never ended.

The minibus that carried us out to the beaches was packed with tourists, most of them older couples with cameras hanging around their necks, most not American. Me and Matt squeezed onto a narrow bench near the back. The bus went to Sword Beach first. We got out and looked down over the bluff. The wind was crisp, and I put my letter jacket back on. The brochure talked about all the troops that had landed there, Canadians and Brits at Sword, Juno and Gold, Americans farther on.

It shook me, the spare stretches of sand and the rocky bluffs, and the conical black roofs on the white stone houses in the distant villages. It was picture-postcard pretty, but the emptiness was loud. You didn't need movie special effects, the *Saving Private Ryan* and *Band of Brothers* pillbox bunkers and tracer bullets and bursting spits of dirt. The quiet and space said it all.

We wandered around Omaha Beach, into the bunkers and machine-gun nests. As a kid, I would have been imagining myself a soldier, maybe even playing war. Dodging behind walls and charging through doorways, tossing grenades into machine-gun nests. But me and Matt just drifted from spot to spot, kind of reverential.

Up the way, past the giant Battle Monument, was the American Cemetery. It was just rows and columns, rows and columns, of white crosses, sometimes a Star of David. I'd seen it a hundred times before in pictures, but you just don't know. You just don't know what it's like. All those crosses and stars.

James W. Smiley, Pvt 116 *Inf* 29 *Div, Omaha, Nebraska, b. March* 17, 1926–*d. June* 6, 1944.

Draper A. Conway, Pvt 16 *Inf* 1 *Div, Lynn, Massachusetts, b. October* 27, 1922–*d. June* 6, 1944.

Arthur L. Rose, Sgt 505 *Inf* 32 *Abn Div, Fairfield, Connecticut, b. January* 4, 1925–*d. June* 6, 1944.

The brochure read: *They died defending freedom and democracy.*

Matt said, "Coaches always talk about blitzes and lobbing bombs and taking no prisoners." He moved from one grave to the next. "But this...what your father does... now that's for real."

I broke away from him then, wandered off by myself. Because...well...I just did. And a few rows on, there was a crucifix and the guy's birthdate was the same as my pops. No lie. September 7. And no lie, his first name was the same. John.

Jack, my Mama called him.

No lie.

Suddenly Matt was there beside me, and he was like, "Hey, you all right? Free?"

"My old man, he's dead, you know." My voice, the words spilling out of me, was like a confession. "In Iraq. They blew him up. An IED. He was riding in a Humvee, him and his team, going to train some new guys or some such. And he wasn't even a combat soldier, just a jet-engine mechanic. I mean, he was a *mechanic*, man."

There was an old couple a few rows over, necklace cameras and all, and they were just staring.

"We had a game the Friday after the casualty-notification officer came to tell us. A big game, to make the playoffs. Ain't none bigger."

I tried to look at Matt as I said it, but I couldn't.

"I played the fucking game, man."

I got my hands free of my pockets and wiped my face, the snot that was at my nose.

"Mama ain't been to church in I don't know how long, Pops sure as shit didn't go, but she's steady going now, with my Grandma Jessie and Auntie Constance in New Orleans. Like that makes one bit of difference, you know? And..."

I didn't know what more to say.

We'd buried a casket, just a metal box with an American flag draped over it, whatever remained inside too far gone for viewing. Taps and a twenty-one-gun salute. Mama behind a black veil, Tookie's face in her shoulder and Tina on her lap. Tookie couldn't stop crying. A colonel in dress blues gave me the triangle of folded flag.

Remembering the funeral now, on that beach in France, I wiped the water off my face, then twisted my class ring free. I laid it at the base of John Wilson Smith's white crucifix, and I took a knee. I crossed my heart with a finger like you see people do in Notre Dame. I didn't really say a prayer, because I didn't know what more there was to say. I just knelt there.

When I opened my eyes, Matt was kneeling beside me. He rose when I rose, then followed me to the minibus. We sat at the rear and waited for the tour guide to lead all the old couples back and for the bus to return us to Caen.

On the ride there, the bus twisting along the beachside roads, Matt said, "You did good, leaving your ring there." He hunched his neck into his collar. "It's just so tacky and gaudy..."

And I busted up. He was laughing too.

FREE

It was pretty late when we finally got back to the museum. The sun had dropped, and the temperature with it. Buses ran on a reduced service on weekends, so we had to wait forty-some minutes for the one to take us to the highway. Once out there, Matt leaned toward the road, thumb out. Soon he was actually in it, on a knee, his hands together, like a plea. The cars just zipped by.

Being a Saturday evening, traffic was thin, almost nothing, and it felt like hours passed before anyone stopped. They dropped us twenty kilometers up the road. Each lift was trifling like that, just a bunch of short ones, and with each one the time got later and the traffic thinner. Some cars taunted us by riding their horns—*beeeep!*—

as they passed. Eventually, almost no cars came by at all, just semis. We tried to wave some down, like we had an emergency or something. Nobody stopped.

I glanced at my cell. It was one in the morning.

"We're not getting back tonight," Matt said. "I'm a moron! Hitchhiking to Normandy on our free day. I thought it would be easy."

But I was like, "Bullshit. Even if we have to walk, we're back tonight."

We hadn't eaten since the crepes at lunch. I was starving, so I knew Matt must be too, but we had the Caïmans the next day—we *had* to get back that night! I took off at a clip.

The highway crossed a small country road, and a sign on it said that some town called Gaillon was three kilometers away. Symbols showed there were hotels and restaurants and a chateau. "Let's head there," I told him. "We'll take the train."

We got to Gaillon by one thirty. It was really just a big village, all asleep, everything closed, no lights but that of the streetlights. Road signs showed that the train station was in the next village over, Aubevoye, two more kilometers away, so we kept walking.

The station was tiny, closed but not locked. A few bums slept on or under benches, using wadded newspaper as pillows and unfolded ones as sheets. The departure board above the ticket window said the next eastbound for Paris wasn't until six forty.

"*Merde!*" Matt said.

"Buck up, laddie," I told him, but he didn't laugh.

"What do we do?" he said.

The bums smelled, the whole place smelled, and we were tired and hungry and needing to get home. I did the only thing I knew to do: I started going through the trashcans. I handed him some wrinkled-up newspaper and kept some for myself.

"Five-star accommodations," I said.

I left a text instead of calling Georges and Françoise, saying I was staying the night at Matt's place and for them not to worry. Matt did the same with Juliette. We stretched out on the cold concrete floor, away from the others and near the ticket window. I rolled onto my side, curled up in a ball and laid my head on my arm, like that would help make it more comfortable.

The six-forty train came through on time. The ticket window was still closed, so we bought tickets from the conductor when he passed. Matt was a wreck—a total wreck!—dark circles under his eyes and his hair all over the place. "Don't say anything to Moose," he said.

Duh.

"What a day to be playing a game," he said. "If I can throw a few scores early, maybe we can build a lead and we'll be all right."

Fifteen guys at practice all week, Mobylette hurt and Matt looking like crap, and the Caïmans the second-ranked team after the Jets.

"Yeah," I said. "Maybe."

Matt dozed off in his seat. Not me. The adrenaline was already flowing. It hadn't really stopped since the night before. Going both ways, offense and defense, returning punts and kickoffs, whatever—it didn't matter, I had to be on. I had done squat all season. I *had* to be on.

I felt queasy and dead-legged in the locker room before the game, and I wasn't sure if it was the trip to Caen or just normal pre-game jitters. Forty or so players had turned up. Every one of us was in his own private place. Some rocked music under headphones, half dressed; others played grab-ass with their neighbors. It was just a way to quash the nerves. Sidi sat in a folding chair, off by himself in a corner of the room. Matt was snoozing in the other corner, a towel over his face. Nobody questioned it.

Moose, across the way, caught my eye. He sat fully suited up already, his helmet on the floor beside his foot, which hammered up and down. He nodded toward Matt, then crossed to him.

When I got there, he nudged Matt with his toe. Matt lifted the towel. His eyes were groggy, and he looked surprised.

Moose addressed me and Matt but loud enough for all to hear. "Listen, the other night was messed up. You regret it, I regret it, but the team is more important than any petty crap."

I couldn't tell if Moose was being straight up or just saying it for the benefit of the team, but Matt gave Moose a thumbs-up so I was all in too, nodding, yeah.

I looked toward where Sidi sat. He looked away.

We went out as a unit. The Caïmans were already on the field, stretching in rows. And there was their Canadian linebacker, on the sideline while the rest warmed up. A big kid, hawking me, checking me out.

None of the other Diables Rouges looked at the Caïmans. We took a lap around the field like always, in a tight knot of players, the pace slow, the pack pushing inward toward a center, Moose and Matt at the front, grunt-growling on the offbeat of our trot, the rest of us silent.

"Hunh," step-step-step, "Hunh," step-step-step, "Hunh," step-step-step.

Moose didn't stop after the first lap like usual. We took a second lap, the gathering pressure to sustain that slow pace in unison upping the intensity of the moment, the intensity of Moose's grunt-growling.

"Hunnnh! Hunnnh! Hunnnh!"

After the second lap, Moose barked orders, shepherding us into lines to stretch. I hustled indoors instead, the movement in my stomach so violent I couldn't believe it was only nerves.

I got back just after the coin toss. Matt signaled to the sideline for the kickoff-return team. We all huddled together around Moose, the coaches over by the benches, discussing final adjustments or some such.

"To them, we're the sorry Diables Rouges from the projects of Villeneuve," Moose said. "Niggers and filthy Arabs!"

"*Racailles*!" Matt joined in.

"I challenge each of you to represent this place we're from," Moose said. "Each of you!"

I broke before he'd even done and went out to my spot on the goal line. The Caïmans, in bright white, stretched from 40 to 40. Some shifted from foot to foot. Some hopped in place. All glared my way. I looked past them, up into the filling stands, at all the people filing in, their eyes on me. There was no noise, really, just a background buzzing.

I don't know if it's right, but for me stadiums are sacred, as close to church as I understand. Even here, at the Beach. I stood there at the goal line, thinking on Private John Wilson Smith, that grave in Normandy. And I thought on Pops.

The Caïmans stilled as I caught the opening kickoff, blew through a seam, then bounced out and sprinted past, away, running down their sideline. Touchdown!

Diables Rouges 7, Caïmans 0.

And it was on. I picked off their quarterback three times in the first half—my first interceptions of the season—and Matt did just like he'd said he would: he threw a couple of quick scores. It was 21–0 at the midway point.

Matt sat in the third quarter. I went in at halfback. My first carry, I deked the Canadian backer, left him lumbering after me as I turned the corner. Forty-some yards later, it was 28–0.

Me and Matt didn't even play the fourth quarter. Coach Le Barbu was carrying his cell phone on his belt, and I asked if I could borrow it. I texted Mama: **Big win 2day. 3 INTs.** I knew she'd read it to Tookie and Tina.

A text came back: **For real? Yeah boiiii!**

We were only one win away from qualifying for the Under-20s championship game.

Matt stood at the water table, helmet and shoulder pads off.

"Number two in the rankings," I told him. "Despite yesterday."

"No fear of success this afternoon."

"Or of failure."

"The pressure to produce," he said, all smiles. "It's why we play."

DIABLES ROUGES (4–1) V. ARGONAUTES (3–2)
APRIL 11

MATT

This pressure to produce. *Merde!*

The scoreboard clock clicked down to 00:00, closing the first half. *VISITEURS* 10, *ARGONAUTES* 7. We had the lead, but they had the edge.

Our opponents, the Argonautes of Aix-en-Provence, were every bit as tough as the Jets. More so, even. Two-time former national champs, the Argos had totally manhandled the Jets a few weeks after we'd lost to them, winning by three touchdowns. But then they got over-confident or something and got spanked by the lousy Mousquetaires, and the next week they lost a squeaker to the Caïmans, 8–7.

The winner in the match between the Argos and us qualified for the final at the historic Stade Jean-Bouin in Paris the following weekend, against the Jets, who'd already clinched first place by dint of their 5–1 record.

Coach Thierry had me play safety to open the game and instructed me to stay deep and mirror the Argos QB, an American who was All-State in high school in Pennsylvania but who couldn't qualify academically for an NCAA scholarship (the dumb ass). The American QB kept looking me off, and their little receivers ran all over the field, our guys chasing after them like those bumbling cops in old silent movies. Twice, Argo receivers dropped passes in the end zone; otherwise we would have been down by two scores.

Free and I headed toward the locker room, where Coach Thierry was surely going to ream us out in his halftime speech. The Argonautes shared a pitch with the local professional rugby club; it had a scoreboard, covered stands and proper seats. Argo fans, milling in the stretches of grass beside the stands, stared at us when they heard our cleats clacking over the concrete walkway.

"What do you call it?" Free said in English. "A self-fulfilling prophecy?"

It had been a nine-hour bus ride down to Aix. We'd taken an overnighter, a *car-couchette,* but instead of sleeping, all the guys had goofed off the whole way, until around daybreak. Since then, everybody had been dragging and out of sync.

"It's on us," I told him, "on you and me. The season rides on it."

» » » »

Free and our DB coach, Celestin, made an adjustment for the second half, shifting to five DBs—the strategy we used against the Anges Bleus—and their French QB didn't know what to do against it. Their offense bogged down in the third quarter.

But ours didn't pick up either with me behind center. The Argos middle linebacker—number 9, a big tough English-Canadian kid who played in the same league I did in Montreal—acted as if the fact that his team back home had eliminated mine from the playoffs last season gave him bragging rights now. He pointed at me before each play and screamed over the crowd noise, "O-ver. Ra-ted." He mimicked my cadence: "Set-hut! Hut-hut! Hut!"

"*Allez*, Mathieu!" Moose chastised me in the huddle during our fourth drive of the third quarter, in what was shaping up to be another three-and-out. "Don't let him get in your head."

"He's not in my head!" I shot back. And to the rest, huddled around me: "Come on! Pick it up, *les gars*!"

But the big bastard clearly was in my head.

Coach Thierry sent in a play-action pass. I called a fake audible at the line to try to confuse number 9, to get him out of his game. He didn't buy the play-action to Mobylette and charged after me. As I scrambled away (I didn't remember him being so fast!), he stripped the ball from my grasp and scooped it up, with nobody between him and the end zone.

Diables Rouges 10, Argonautes 14.

I didn't even look at Moose as I headed back to our bench. Free knew me well enough to know to leave me alone.

It came down to this: our ball with 2:41 left on the clock in the fourth quarter and seventy-three yards of turf between us and a rematch with the Jets for the Under-20s championship. I called one of our two remaining timeouts.

"Are you out of your mind?" Coach Thierry yelled as I jogged over to the bench.

Freeman joined the other coaches on the edge of the playing field. Coach Thierry was chiding me—"Keep your head in it; we can't afford to waste timeouts!"—when Free said, "Think the guys can handle the no-huddle?"

We'd never done it before.

"If we limit the plays," I said.

"To which ones, for example?" Coach Le Barbu asked.

"The floods. Middle- and out-cuts," I said, faking a confidence I wasn't really feeling.

"Add a go route," Free said, "to keep the safeties honest."

"It can work," said Coach Le Barbu. "Sure. Why not?"

"Because we've never practiced it!" Coach Thierry said.

I looked at Freeman, who was smiling.

"Live and learn," he said in English.

"Or crash and burn," I said.

I turned to Coach Thierry, looked him in the eye and said, "*Ça pourrait marcher.*"—This could work.

He met my eyes, then dropped his own and paced away. But just as quickly he turned on his heels and strode back, clapping his hands. "*Vas-y*, boy! Go get 'em."

Number 9 eyed me the length of my jog back to our huddle.

When I got there, Moose was in the middle of a pep talk. "They're doing the same as the cops back home. They're trying to test you. So whatever they say in these last few minutes, whatever they do"—he was looking straight at Sidi—"whether it's an insult or a cheap shot, keep your cool."

"All right, listen up." I explained that we were going no-huddle, to line up in Ace and hustle back and reset after each play, whether we completed the pass or not. I gave the receivers the crude code I'd devised on the jog out. If I tapped the ear hole of my helmet, it was the deep outside flood; the top of my head, the middle flood; my thigh, the all-go route. I repeated it one more time. "No improvising. If you forget what to do, just run your man off."

The ref stepped next to me, tapped his watch. "Twenty seconds," he warned.

"It's do or die," I said, looking one by one through the face mask of each guy around me. "Play fast. Play hard. The snap is always on one. *Vous êtes prêts!*"

"Break!" they responded.

Sidi had been pretty quiet all day, not making mistakes but not making plays either. My dad says a leader makes his players see what they *can* be rather than what they are. I jogged over to Sidi, on the flank, even though seconds were ticking off the clock.

"You've been wanting to make up for the Anges Bleus game," I told him. "Here's your chance. I'm looking for you."

I patted him on the butt and jogged back, looking over at number 9.

"You know where I'm going," I told him in English.

I tapped the top of my head and caught the snap, fired back early. (My center, Jorge, was clearly wound up.) Number 9 didn't even try to read the play; he sprinted right toward Sidi. But Sidi curled under him—I waited for him to clear—and made a nice catch in front of their safety. An eleven-yard gain.

"What you gonna do?" I screamed at number 9, doing my best Freeman. "You knew where I was going and still couldn't do nothing about it!"

I hustled back into position, let the receivers get back into place, then tapped the top of my helmet again. Jorge was calmer; he waited for my cadence before snapping the ball. I dropped back two steps, reading the safety, but none of my receivers came clear and number 9 was blitzing, so I just let fly, overthrew everybody and killed the clock.

"That's more like it," number 9 said, standing over me.

I was on the ground, my left shoulder smarting, but I hollered back, "What you gonna do? I'm going to number 87 this next play. What you gonna do?"

The ref broke us up. He warned 9 to be careful of drawing a late-hit penalty, him and me still jawing at each other.

Sidi was suddenly by my side. "Be cool, *mec*," hot-headed Sidi said to me. "Be cool."

I got back into position behind Jorge. The scoreboard clock read 2:01. The Argos dragged, slow to line up. I patted my ear hole so that as soon as the ref whistled the ball live, we could get another play off while they were in disarray.

I wanted to hit Moose, our number 87, so that I stayed in number 9's head. But both the corner and the safety keyed on Moose, number 9 camping in the lane, cutting off the possibility of even a miraculous throw and catch (which I realized I was about to try anyway, still too focused on showing up number 9).

I saw Manu, our backside slot receiver, making his break. It was a long throw, clear across the field and only good for a few yards, but he made the catch. The clock doesn't stop in college rules for the two-minute warning, but Manu got out of bounds, killing it at 1:43. We were still only at our own 36-yard line. I called our guys back into the huddle.

"Catch your breath," I told them. "All right, two plays." I called our bread-and-butter play of the season: "Split left, flare left, tight-end delay right. For the second, shotgun draw 43."

It was risky, as both plays would keep the ball in the middle of the field, keeping the clock alive, but hopefully the Argos wouldn't expect it, and we'd get big gains. Regardless, we'd have to use our last timeout after.

"On one, on one. *Vous êtes prêts!*"

"Break!"

As we lined up, I told Mobylette, "After you get tackled on the draw"—the second play—"find the ref and call a timeout immediately, even before you give him the ball."

"*Moi pas plaqué*"—Me not get tackled, the cocky bastard said, his smile bright against his dark face.

The first play worked like a charm. Number 9 charged on a blitz, I lobbed the ball right over his head to our tight end, Jean-Marc, and we gained thirteen yards and a first down.

We hurried to line up, the Argos dragging—1:27, 1:26, 1:25—and I gave a false signal, tapping my ear hole. Number 9 clearly picked up on it. When he sprinted out toward Moose on the snap, I slipped the ball into Mobylette's belly and he was off, backside.

Boy, could he run!

He juked the other linebacker and bounced outside. The safety pushed him out of bounds after a nice gain, all the way to their 35.

He hustled back to line up, and I saw his smile before I caught his words. "Me permit him get me," he said, "but save last timeout."

The clock was stopped at 1:02. I felt myself breathing hard, but the others looked spry. *They were on!* I didn't huddle us up. I tapped my thigh, the all-go route, to keep their DBs honest. And who knew? Maybe one of my receivers would get open.

None did, but as I was reading number 9, I lost sight of my backside, and their blitzing corner tagged me. The ball came loose. I didn't see this—all I saw was turf—but I heard their sideline and fans hurrah. Then I heard our guys hurrah, and I looked up, and Claude Benayoun was lying on the ball.

The clock was winding down—00:50, 00:49, 00:48…

We'd lost seven yards. I patted my ear hole as our guys lined up, took the snap. The Argos thought this meant Moose, so I went the opposite way again, to Manu. An eleven-yard gain, back to the 31-yard line, and the clock was stopped with thirty-three seconds left.

I patted the top of my head, took the snap. Sidi cleared number 9, but the safety closed hard, so I dropped the ball over his head to Moose. He made a good catch of my wobbly throw. His man tackled him right away, in the middle of the field.

I called our last timeout.

We had a first down, but that didn't matter. With only nineteen seconds left, we'd have time for two plays, max, to get the ball the last seventeen yards into the end zone.

Coach Thierry, Coach Le Barbu, Freeman and the other coaches waited for me in a group on the sideline. The rest of the team stood not far behind, wound tight but quiet. The stands were still too.

"Well, what do you think?" Coach Thierry asked.

I was hoping he'd tell me. I turned toward Free.

"Take him on," he said in English. "For real. The Canadian backer is itching to make a play." Then, in French (though the coaches had surely understood his English), he said, "Try the play-action he blew up earlier." The play he scored on. "He'll bite on the fake to Mobylette this time."

I looked at Coach Thierry, at Coach Le Barbu. Neither said anything.

"Let's do it," I said.

The huddle was silent when I returned. Moose, Mobylette, Jorge, Sidi.

"Who wants it?" I said.

Nobody responded. Nobody moved.

"Who wants it!"

"*Moi!*"

"*À moi le ballon!*"

They were all talking at once now.

"Settle down," I told them, and they did. "Number 9 thinks he's hot shit, but he's the weak link. His cockiness is his weakness. We're going right at him. Double T, motion, inside loops. I need protection, and I need you guys"—I looked to my receivers—"to get open in the end zone."

I paused, took a deep breath.

"We're out of timeouts, so if we don't get in, everybody hustle back and line up fast. We'll run the same play again, only flip the formation."

I took another breath.

"Okay," I said. "On one. *Vous êtes prêts!*"

"Break!"

Number 9 aimed his gaze at me as we lined up. He wasn't saying anything, just staring. He cheated up, showing blitz, and their strong safety cheated over onto Moose. That should open up the seam on the left of the goalpost, where Sidi was supposed to end up. If I had time.

I didn't really know what was happening as it was happening, just that it happened. Mobylette sold the fake so well that number 9 tagged him, grunting, "Damn!" when he realized he'd been had. The line must have been blocking well because it was like a 7-on-7 passing drill. I had all the time in the world, no pressure. I watched the corner and safety double up on Moose. I watched Sidi break behind them. I saw the pass—a really nice, tight spiral—sail right at him. Sidi raised his hands and cradled it into his body, then fell backward into the end zone.

The final seconds ticked by—00:03, 00:02, 00:01...The referee whistled the end of the game.

The roaring faded in then. All the screaming and cheering. Even from some of their fans, so spectacular was the ending.

Our guys rushed the field, singing and dancing. "*Olé! Olé-Olé-Olé!*"

Moose grabbed me up in his arms. Claude, Jorge, Paco and some others lifted Sidi onto their shoulders. On the sideline, Free and Coach Thierry were jumping up and down.

The Argonautes. A few stood about, shell-shocked. Most left the pitch, heads hanging, without shaking our hands. The linebacker, number 9, just sat on the field, his shoulders jerking, visibly sobbing.

Sidi was suddenly beside me. He was crying too.

"*Merci*, Matt," he said, one arm around my neck. "*Merci!*"

The showers in the stadium's locker room were enormous compared to the ones at the Beach, ten or twelve jets along facing walls. Free and I pulled trainers' tables under the two at the far end, took off our clothes, opened the valves full blast and lay down. We stayed under the hot stream a long time, neither him or me speaking, guys coming and going, still dancing and singing. "*Olé! Olé-Olé-Olé!*"

Sometime later, Coach Thierry poked his head in. "*Eh-oh, grouilles-toi*," he said—Hustle now. "We're loading the bus."

I must have fallen asleep. Freeman had already left.

Leaving Aix, it was like I only then noticed the landscape, fields and fields that were purple with lavender. The *car-couchette* wasn't any more comfortable than it had been the night before, on the way down. The metallic seat frame pressed into my back, and the AC was fussy, either too cold or too hot.

Free, who was in the sleeper above mine, leaned over the bunk's edge. "Dang, Matt," he said. "We're number two in the country. We're playing in the final."

"Dang," I replied.

Moose, in the next sleeper down, leaned into the aisle. "What else did you expect!" he said, dismissive. He was all bravado now. Everybody was. We were dead tired, but all the sleepers buzzed with chatter and shrieks and laughter.

"*Et les gars*," he called to the rest. "These '*Ricains* have no faith. They think we're just *racaille* and *voyous*"—scum and thugs—he teased.

Freeman shot back. "Thugs? You guys are soft." He used the wrong word for *soft*—*doux* instead of *mou*—but everybody understood. "*Non*, it's me. I am *voyou*." And he popped out of his bunk and into the aisle, throwing gang signs with his hands and starting into this old rap by the French group Assassin:

Le futur que nous réserve-t-il?

De moins en moins de nature, de plus en plus de villes!

He couldn't rap to save his life, especially in French, but the guys were hooting. Moose too. Free and Moose seemed to have gotten closer, despite the rough start.

I leaned back in my bunk. The championship game was one week away. And after that we'd be leaving, Free and me. Me, back to Montreal—to Orford for summer school. Business classes.

I pulled out my cell and texted my dad. **DR 17-Aix 10.** I added that I'd thrown the winning TD as time ran out.

No response. Maybe he was out at the cabin or his phone was off.

MATT

The Monday afternoon after the Argonautes win, Aïda texted me from the Louvre. She'd texted me the week before too, and she and I had met at the Fontaine des Innocents at Les Halles and sat and talked. It turned out that she came down to the city on her own sometimes when there wasn't school, without Sidi or anyone else knowing. (She said Sidi would throw a fit and tell their father.) She went to museums or to public gardens to stroll and read or to the Centre Pompidou, like Freeman and I did.

I texted an excuse to Free, who I was supposed to get together with, and met up with Aïda instead. She had on the red-and-white headscarf—the one she had taken off under the Étoile to show me her hair. But instead of going into the Louvre, we crossed the street to the Pont des Arts, the steel-and-wood pedestrian bridge that stretches from the museum over to the Institut de France. Free and I would come to the Pont sometimes. Young people would be lounging around, smoking and talking; someone might be playing a guitar. This afternoon, it was quiet.

Aïda and I didn't say much either, just casual chat, then we were quiet too. We sat on the wooden planks in the middle of the bridge, our backs against the metal railing, the Seine coursing underneath. In front of us was the Île Saint-Louis, hints of the spires of Notre Dame between the rooftops.

"I saw a movie earlier," she said finally.

"Oh yeah. Which one?"

She said the name, but I didn't recognize it. "It was about a girl," she said. "Or a young woman, really. Eighteen. She comes from a good family—very bourgeois, you know—and she does well in school and has good friends."

"And she's unhappy, of course."

"No," Aïda said. "Actually, she's not. But she prostitutes herself all the same. She makes an online ad and meets these random men in a hotel near Montmartre."

"Wow."

"I know."

I couldn't tell if she was saying all this for the shock value or what.

"The girl isn't outraged or rebellious or making a point," Aïda said. "It's just what she does. And watching, I felt like I wasn't supposed to feel sad either."

"Did you?" I asked. "Feel sad, I mean."

"Just kind of empty." She looked over at me, then away again, uncharacteristically reserved. "And I guess a little sad too."

One of the tourist boats, a Bateau Mouche, glided by beneath the bridge, every row full of tilted-up red faces, looking at the old architecture. A few seemed to catch sight of us.

"So what happens in the movie?" I asked.

"A man is murdered, and everything gets complicated," she said.

Then she added, "Listen, I have to get back," and it was only then that I noted the fading light. The sun was dropping toward the rooftops so fast you could almost see it moving.

I walked her toward Les Halles, where she would catch the RER. Foot traffic had picked up with the end of the workday. We passed beside the Saint-Eustache church, where skateboarders in baggy pants and knit caps backsided and frontsided around the park benches. One did a railslide down a freestanding metal bannister, his board *screeeeeeech*ing. A little farther on was this boulder, at least ten feet high, sculpted to look like a huge head resting lightly in the palm of a stone hand. A couple lounged in the cupped hand, the woman whispering in the guy's ear, the guy laughing.

I pointed to the church. "It's a mixture of Gothic and Renaissance." I'd read that in a guidebook, *Le Guide du Routard*. "Freeman says it's ugly."

"Really?" she said. "It's my favorite."

"Mine too. It looks like a giant ship, its sails catching the wind, bearing down on the Forum."

I hadn't read that. I was just winging it.

"That's what I like about it too." She pointed from the church to the metal-and-neon shopping mall. "Two worlds colliding."

We took the long escalator down into the Forum, where the RER station was, me in front, her behind, so that people in a rush could get past. I could almost feel Aïda's breath on the back of my neck. Midway she laid a hand on my shoulder. I stared down into the fluorescent-lit dark, then rested my hand over hers. We rode in silence like that, still as statues.

I heard a muffled drumbeat, Bob Marley's "Revolution."

"Funky ringtone," I told her.

I've always loved Bob Marley. Before my parents split up, we would take family vacations in the Islands during the winter, and her ringtone reminded me of dancing to his music on the beach in Jamaica with a girl named Lora, whose older sister worked at the resort. I also remembered my mom on that particular trip sitting me down in the hotel for a talk. She warned me to be careful "playing tease with the locals," and I told her she was being racist.

"*Putain*," I heard Aïda say. She was reading the display on her phone. "I need to get back to Villeneuve. Now." She dropped my hand and took off at a clip.

I struggled through the crowd, trying to keep up. She didn't stop until she got to the ticket turnstile at the RER station.

"Wait," I said. "What's going on?"

"It was from Sidi. Monsieur Oussekine just found out about Moussa's trouble at school."

I had to jog my memory. "From three months ago? Him breaking back in?"

"Sidi says he's going to ship Moussa off to Algeria." Her expression was dead serious.

"Would he really?"

"On God's head," said Aïda. "To live with a great-uncle he's never even met. Marc Lebrun and Yazid are going to talk to Monsieur Oussekine right now."

We inserted our tickets into the machine, and I followed her through a crush of people to the platform.

"What kind of parents would send their kid off to another country?" I said.

Aïda looked at me the same way Moose had that night on the Champs-Élysées, when he called me "so white" —more disbelieving than disappointed but a little bit of both. As if my mouth spoke things on its own that the rest of me couldn't possibly be thinking.

"Parents who work sixteen hours a day to put food on the table, that's who. Fathers who are tired of seeing their sons screw up in school and who are afraid they'll do the same with the rest of their lives. Mothers who want a better future for their daughters and who understand they'll only attain it here if they learn the discipline of there."

The RER train rolled into the station. Aïda pushed forward.

"My parents would do the same to me," she said. "They've already threatened Sidi."

The train was crowded, but we were able to get two seats next to a window. It was only six stops to Villeneuve. The buzzer signaled that the doors were closing, and I texted Moose, typing with both thumbs. **Are you ok?**

He answered instantly. **Got any packing tips?**

Aïda stared out the window. I did too. I looked at the forest of high-rises, trees in blossom in between, as we came out from underground and realized that spring was really under way. Ten minutes later we were in the streets of Villeneuve, headed toward the clubhouse. Our arms kind of rubbed as we walked, and as we rounded the corner by the Greek sandwich shop, I was like, *Go on, wuss!* and I slipped my hand into hers.

She jerked free, like my hand had shot her with a jolt of electricity.

"Not here."

"I'm sorry," I said, and I stared at the high-rises, at the faces passing by. I felt kind of embarrassed.

But I also didn't know what to make of her reaction. I mean, she was the one who had made the first move, on the escalator in the Forum.

We crossed the big cement courtyard. A group of players, six or seven of them, were gathered in front of the clubhouse. Yasmina and Sidi spotted us and headed our way. "Marc and Yazid just left with Moose," Yasmina said.

"To meet with his father," Sidi added. He looked at us kind of suspiciously.

Aïda shot back, "Why aren't you with them?"

"They didn't want me there," Sidi said, looking suddenly sheepish, and I could see in his face the little boy he still was behind all the bravado and the spleefs.

"Yaz said Sidi had already contributed more than enough toward Moose's cause," Yasmina said, and I laughed.

Aïda didn't.

Neither did Sidi. "I'm sick of being tagged as the screwup!"

"You know I love you," Yasmina said, "but come on. You do have a knack for making messes."

"And no demonstrated ability for cleaning them up," said Aïda.

"So anyway," I said, trying to help Sidi out, "what do we do now?"

We all looked at one another.

"Wait," Aïda said.

We went into the clubhouse and sat around the conference table, talking and playing backgammon. Aïda mostly ignored me. She leaned in toward Yasmina and whispered stuff, all conspiratorial.

I stepped outside and dialed Moose's number. I got his voice mail after the first ring and left a message: "Your phone must be off. Call me when you get this."

I texted Free: **Moose getting sent to Algeria.**

He called right away. "For real? He's out for the final?"

"He's out for the rest of his life," I said. Then I explained everything.

"So what do we do?" Free said.

"What can we do?"

I wanted to ask his advice about this stuff with Aïda, but I didn't. I told him I'd call later, after I knew more about Moose.

When I got back inside, Sidi was on the phone, talking to his mom or dad. He hung up and told Aïda, "We have to get back for supper."

"Me too," Yasmina said, gathering her things. "I should be going."

Out in front of the building, Aïda turned to her brother. "Go on," she said. "Tell Father I'll be there soon."

Sidi looked from her to me and back again. "How long will you be? I can wait for you."

"You think I need you to watch over me?" she snapped.

He dropped his eyes and shuffled away.

We took the same route to the train station, only in reverse. I made sure we weren't touching at all.

"So what's up?" I asked.

"Nothing is up. Can't I walk you to the train station without something being up?"

We covered the last blocks in silence, passed the turnstile and followed the *Trains to Paris* sign to the platform. The electric board indicated that the next one would arrive in two minutes.

"Better start talking," I said, tapping my watch.

The station was empty. Aïda went to the far end of the platform. I followed.

"I just wanted to apologize," she said.

"For what?"

"For shaking your hand off earlier. I didn't mean to be rude, it's just that..."

She looked toward the ground.

I said, "What?"

"You know." She was standing square in front of me now. "I don't want your being with me to be about some rich kid slumming."

"Look at who my friends are, Aïda." The board said I had one minute. "Don't you know me well enough to know I'm not like that?"

"But Matt, I live here and you don't. Your mother runs a company, and my father sweeps the street. When you go back to Montreal, I'll still be here."

I heard the train coming. Our faces were only inches apart.

"I have to be able to trust that you have my back," she said.

Have her back? I thought I did. I was certainly trying to. Hers. Moose's. Sidi's. But I began to wonder if I even knew what this meant.

It made me think about Jamaica, those family trips to the Islands, what my mom had accused me of—*playing tease with the locals*. We'd stay a week and I'd run around with the Jamaican kids, listening to reggae, swimming or messing around on the beach, and I remember thinking of myself as Jamaican. But I'd never really stopped to think how insulting that was. The real Jamaicans didn't look anything like me. No matter how much I hung out with them, no matter what we did together, I'd never be like them. I was one of the others, who came from elsewhere, with dollars in their pockets, for the sun and the ocean, living in a hotel with a pool and a private beach and security guards and loving it. Pathetic.

"I get it," I told her. "You have to believe me that I do."

"Because I don't want to be the silly Arab girl who fell for the rich Canadian who was just visiting."

Up the tracks, the train rounded the corner, closing in.

"You're leaving in, what?" she said. "One week? Two?"

"Classes don't start until September."

"September," she said. "And your mom will let you stay until then?" But she didn't wait for an answer. She took my face between her hands and kissed me. Right there, right on the platform.

The taste of her. Her scent. The faint smell of shampoo. Strawberry.

The train barreled into the station and slid to a stop. She slowly backed away. Then she laughed.

"This," she said, pointing back and forth between us, "won't be a walk in the park. I can be difficult."

"So I've learned."

People got off the train, and I leaped on. I sat next to the window beside where she stood on the platform. I laid my hand against the window. When she did the same, we both burst into laughter. I couldn't hear her through the glass, but I read her lips: "Corny," she said as the train started to roll.

I watched her grow smaller and then completely disappear.

I texted Moose before I lost reception underground.

How did meeting go?

My phone rang the second we resurfaced, five stops later, at Port-Royal. "Yaz and Marc convinced my father to not send me back to the *bled*," Moose told me.

"That's awesome!"

"Under one condition," he continued. "I have to quit the team."

FREE

Me and Matt met at Les Halles the next afternoon. He was sitting on the lip of the Fontaine des Innocents as I walked up.

"You sure this is a good idea?" I asked.

"It can't hurt."

"If Monsieur Lebrun and Yaz didn't get anywhere, what can you and me accomplish?"

"You underestimate my charm and powers of persuasion."

We had our big bags with our gear so we could go straight to practice after, but I was dressed fly, in black slacks and a white shirt.

Matt busted on me. "Did you get a side job as a waiter?"

"Oh snap," I said, and I gave him the hand.

He pointed to a florist's shop. "For Moose's mom."

A little old lady sold us the *Délice du Printemps*, which meant "spring delight." It was a bouquet of yellow tea roses, white lilies, pink gerberas and blue lisianthus. (She had to explain this to us; I don't know yellow tea roses from Guns N' Roses.) On the train, we sat silent, me holding the bouquet. I didn't tell Matt this, but I hadn't ever been in a Muslim's home before. Ever. I didn't know what to expect, and I was kind of nervous behind it, especially as we were trekking up there to tell a grown man how to raise his son.

It was seven floors up, and the elevator was broken. The cement stairwell reeked of piss. With our huge bags, me and Matt were in a sweat and working for breath by the time we reached their door. In the hallway outside was a line of shoes and sandals. Matt slipped out of his, and when I didn't, he nudged me. When my shoes were off, he rang the bell.

A little girl, ten, maybe eleven years old, in a long embroidered shirt and a blue-and-yellow headscarf, opened the door. She yelled back into the apartment, "Moussa, *les américains des Diables*!" Then back to us, beaming: "*Salut, les champions*."

An older lady appeared—Madame Oussekine?—in a high-necked robe that reached the floor and a dark headscarf. "Please, please." She waved us in. Then, kind of scolding: "You should have called to let us know you were coming."

I extended the flowers.

"How lovely! Let me find a vase."

Their living room was long and narrow, with green walls. The ceiling was kind of low, the room kind of tight, with stuff everywhere. There was an oak cabinet with glass doors, filled with old books, colored candles and framed pictures. One was a black-and-white—super old—of a man in an army uniform.

Moose came out from the back, not looking too pleased. "What are you doing here?" he whispered.

"Saving your ass," Matt whispered back.

Before Moose could say anything more, a man appeared at the end of the hallway, tall and lean, in a long white robe and skullcap. Monsieur Oussekine was straight up a replica of Moose, fast-forward forty years, and with a full beard.

"Welcome to my home," he said in a booming voice. It seemed to echo over every other noise in the apartment. But he didn't smile. Kind of the opposite: his face was as quiet as a closed door.

Moose was sort of...submissive in front of his pops. Not like nothing I'd ever seen of him. "Father, meet Mathieu Dumas. His family hosted me in Montreal last summer."

Monsieur Oussekine's face loosened some at that, but not much.

"And this is Freeman Behanzin. He comes from Texas."

He took me in with a glance and waved for us to sit down. Matt and me sat side by side on this old leather sofa, and he took the large chair beside the window. Moose stayed off in the corner, near the hallway. The air was stuffy with the smell of food frying in the kitchen.

"Let me guess," Monsieur Oussekine said. "You're here to try to convince me to let my son stay on the team."

It wasn't a question.

"Yes, sir," Matt said, and then he started in, and it sounded kind of rehearsed. "Like all fathers, I'm sure you know what the—"

Monsieur Oussekine cut him off. "How old are you, son?"

"Eighteen, sir. Well, almost."

"And you propose to lecture me on what's best for my children?"

Matt stared at his shoes.

The girl who'd opened the door carried in this fancy sculpted tray with a copper teapot on it like the one in *Aladdin*. It saved our asses. Monsieur Oussekine took his focus off us and turned it onto the tray. There were these fresh but ridiculously small glasses in a bunch, and he served us mint tea by holding the pot up high, lowering it to the lip of a glass and then moving on to the next one, splashing tea all over the table. I didn't know if we were supposed to raise the cups in a toast or throw them back like movie cowboys do a shot of whiskey. Matt sipped at his, his eyes still fixed on his feet, so I followed his lead—or tried to. The glass was scalding. I put it back down and blew air on my burning fingertips. And we just sat there, looking at one another.

I said, "Moose—I mean, Moussa. He told us you work as an urban technician. For the city of Paris. That must be interesting?"

"Interesting? No. But essential. I'm what the municipality calls a *technicien responsable de la propreté urbaine*."

"Pardon?" I asked.

"I'm a garbage collector."

There was a long silence. Then Monsieur Oussekine broke it with this high-pitched, songlike laugh. It didn't match his voice.

"But Father studied to be a mechanical engineer," Moose jumped in, kind of defensive, "when he still lived in Algiers."

"Yes, yes, that's true," his father said. "In the gas and oil industry. That hasn't meant much here though, and it was a long time ago."

I didn't realize I was staring at a framed medal, over in the oak cabinet beside the picture of the soldier, but Monsieur Oussekine went and got it and laid it on the coffee table. It was a bronze cross with a red-and-white ribbon.

"This catches your eye?" he said. "It was the ticket my father, Moussa's grandfather, paid so that we could come here."

"*Pardon, Monsieur*?" Matt said, looking as baffled as I felt.

"During the war of independence, in our home, in Algeria, my father"—Monsieur Oussekine pointed to the man in the picture—"was a *Harki*."

A *Harki*? But I didn't have to ask because he just went on and explained.

"My father fought for France against the insurgents who would eventually take over Algeria. *Harki* is what these native troops were called." He refilled Matt's glass, with the same up-and-down stroke. "He died in combat."

"The French government," Moose said, his voice rising, "after getting beaten, refused to even admit that a war had been fought. They called it a 'police action,' as though my grandfather had died for nothing."

"No, no, my son," Monsieur Oussekine said. "French citizenship—that's what he got in exchange." He turned to Matt and me. "His sacrifice was our ticket to France."

"*Full* French citizenship?" Moose said, half under his breath.

"My angry son isn't all wrong," said Monsieur Oussekine. "When you look at the life we have here..."

He rose and went to the long window. "This place." He pointed to the surrounding high-rises. "They name the buildings after artists: Balzac, Ravel, Debussy—our own building, Renoir. But even doctors won't come for emergency calls. Tell me, how can you raise a boy correctly in a place like this?"

He wasn't calling us out, but it was like he was saying, *I know why you came around, but step off. Step up out my business.*

But still Matt jumped in. "That's why the Diables Rouges are so important," he said.

Monsieur Oussekine waved him off, then locked his hands behind his back. "School is important, not things that distract from school."

"But we need other outlets," Matt insisted. "Kids like Moussa, they need an outlet. *Especially* in a place like this. That's what the Diables Rouges provide."

But me, I was thinking about Villeneuve and about what Monsieur Oussekine had said. "My father," I said, "he grew up in Chicago."

I stopped myself, trying to figure out how to explain it so they'd understand.

"The West Side, where my father grew up, it's very much like this. Not so different. There were..." I couldn't find the word for *gangs*, so I just said it in English: "*Il y avait des* gangs."

Matt translated: "*Des bandes rivales.*"

"*Il y avait des bandes rivales,*" I said, then continued,

"My father used to tell me that there were gangs and drugs all over, and lots of trouble with the police. Lots of racism, you see."

Monsieur Oussekine stared at me. Moose too.

"He and my mother had me, but they weren't married. You see? They were very young, like Moussa and Mathieu and me, and they had a child, and the one thing that saved him."

I paused. *Saved* him?

"The thing he told me saved him and his new family was the military. Kind of like your father."

"It was his ticket," Monsieur Oussekine said.

"Yes. But he wanted better for me than he had."

I couldn't find the word for *stationed*, so I said it otherwise. "Because of the air force, we resided in San Antonio..."

"In Texas," Matt said.

"We resided in San Antonio, and there were gangs and drugs too, a lot of trouble, and my father was often gone, on duty overseas, and my mother now had my little brother and sister too. My father insisted I play football."

"As an outlet," Matt said, but I said, "No, not as an outlet. For the structure. For the discipline. Because he thought it would help me make better decisions."

Matt jumped in again, and I was glad he did that time, because Monsieur Oussekine was steady staring at me and I didn't know what more to say.

"Maybe sometimes Moussa has made bad decisions. Who doesn't? But the leadership he's learned from the Diables Rouges, the loyalty...He looked out for Sidi, even though he knew it could get him into trouble. Like you yourself look out for Moussa."

Monsieur Oussekine was still staring at me. Not angry like he might have been for me calling him out about his business, but firm all the same. "Your father sounds like a wise man," he said. "He must be very proud."

Proud?

"My father." I pointed to the medal. "He was killed last fall in Iraq." The words just came out. "My father, like your father."

I looked at Monsieur Oussekine, and it was like he heard me saying something I wasn't saying out loud. The thing I didn't know how to say.

"You're afraid he was a sort of *Harki*?" Monsieur Oussekine said. "That he was used by the military and thrown away?"

I didn't know what to say.

He came to the couch, sat beside me. "Your father, my father," he said, "they weren't lackeys. This medal isn't something to be ashamed of, something to hide away in a shoe box in the closet."

He removed it from its case, put it in my hand.

"Touch it."

I ran my fingertip along the cold grain of the metal.

He said, "This coin and ribbon, it's my father, in all his strength. It's the physical embodiment of him, of a man who had the courage to live his convictions."

I returned it, looking away. Not embarrassed. Just…I don't know.

"And Moussa too," I heard Matt say. "He has the courage to live his convictions too."

Matt leaned forward in his seat, and Monsieur Oussekine was listening to him, but his arm was draped over my shoulders. And me, I just looked away.

Matt said, "Moussa is why I'm here, Monsieur Oussekine, in Villeneuve. He had the vision to see what an experience this would be for me. And the courage to look out for me, for Freeman and me, in this place. I, we, his friends, we come to you today because we want to do for Moussa the same that he always does for us."

Monsieur Oussekine didn't respond. He just sat there, his arm draped over my shoulders.

A little bit later, we were in the hallway outside their apartment, me and Matt and Moose. Moose was excited, hugging us and all.

"*Putain, les mecs. Merci*," he said. "*Merci*."

Matt was all smiles too. "I didn't think we could pull it off."

"The things you said!" Moose said to me, but then he stopped, put a hand on my shoulder. "Why didn't you ever tell us?"

I shook my head. I didn't know why I had told them just then. But it felt public finally, Pops's death. Like everybody knew.

It didn't feel wrong though. Doesn't still. Pops's death is part of who I am. I will carry his memory like a medal and ribbon, a ticket to being my best me.

"Your father," I told Moose. "He's great."

FOUR DAYS BEFORE THE UNDER-20s
CHAMPIONSHIP GAME
APRIL 15

MATT

And now Free and I are stranded outside the locked construction site at Villeneuve, some of our teammates arrested and hauled off in a van, Moose and Sidi and Mobylette run off into the night, police cars speeding after them. It's the day after Free and I went to Moose's home, and what we'd fixed the night before with Monsieur Oussekine is all of a sudden completely undone. From that high to this low, just like that.

Four days before the championship!

And where are Moose and Sidi and Mobylette now? And how do Free and I fix it?

My throwing shoulder throbs—sharp and piercing, like something is ripped—from when the police officer yanked me to my feet by my handcuffed hands. Four days before the league championship!

Freeman is saying, "Of course, we won't tell Monsieur Oussekine what just happened..." But he says it half uncertainly, like he's thinking aloud, working his way through something. "Of course not." He turns toward me. "But there'll be Yaz at the *cité*. Or some other *grands frères*. We can tell them. They'll know what to do."

We start toward Moose's building. It's about a ten-minute walk. The road is eerie between lampposts, full of shadows and creepy quiet. And Free and I are quiet too. I don't know what he's thinking, but all I can see in my head is Monsieur Oussekine's face, enraged. Or disappointed. Or first one and then the other. I told him about how great the Diables Rouges were for Moose and what Moose brought to the Diables, and he confided in us about his own father and about his fears for his son, and now...here we are.

Along one stretch of street, all the lights suddenly cut out. The entire neighborhood, in fact. All the lights in all the buildings all around. Pitch-black.

"Dang!" Free says.

Both Free and I freeze. Dogs bark. I can hear a kid crying in the distance. In windows, candles appear, flashlights; here and there, faces look out into the night.

Then, just as suddenly, the streetlights, all the lights, stutter back on.

"Dang," he repeats. "This has been one hell of a day."

» » » »

At Moose's building we come upon a group of *grands-frères*. No Yaz, but one is Mobylette's actual older brother, Khalil; I've seen him at games. They're standing outside, all of them looking around, talking about the blackout.

"*Bonsoir*," I say. "We're friends of Amadou and Moussa, Moussa Oussekine."

One recognizes us. "*Les 'Ricains des Diables Rouges*," he says.

The others place us too. They greet us, shake our hands.

"What's up?" another asks.

"Amadou and Moussa, and Sidi Bourghiba—we were with them. Over by the construction site," I explain. "There were a lot of us."

They listen intently, but I don't know what I'm trying to say.

"The cops came, and they took a bunch of us away," I say.

The *grands frères* all look grave.

Mobylette's brother says, "And Madou?"

"Amadou and Moussa and Sidi," I say, "they ran off."

"Oh, shit," Free says. He sees him first.

We all look in the direction he's looking.

It's Sidi, staggering toward us across the parking lot. His shirt, his pants, everything, all shredded. His skin, great big patches—gone. And it's, like, smoke coming off him.

The *grands frères*, Free and me, we're running to him.

Sidi falls to his knees, his face all blistered and wet, his eyes dark holes against the pink rawness.

Everybody is talking at once.

"What happened?"

"What happened, *mon frère*?"

And the smell.

"Moby..." Sidi is mumbling. "Moussa..."

One of the *grands frères* stays with Sidi, telephoning for help, while the rest of us run through the dark streets over to the electrical substation, Freeman and me following Khalil and the others, and when we get there, four police cars surround the barbed-wire-topped walls, their blue lights pulsing in the night. The cops cluster in small groups near the compound entrance, a couple of the ones from earlier and others in uniform. There's an EDF van too—Éléctricité de France, the French utilities company—

but the technicians just stand there, holding their tools. The police, the EDF guys—nobody is even trying to go in.

The night air bites, but so much heat is coming from the humming substation that I break into a sweat. Skulls and crossbones cover the compound walls. Warning signs. *Danger–High Voltage. Electricity—it's stronger than you.* One painted to look like a tagger wrote it: *STOP! Don't risk your life.*

I don't know what to do. I kind of want to yell out to Moose and Mobylette, to tell them to come out now, that it's okay.

The humming of the electric compound is a loud, metallic whirring. And the crowd keeps growing, people running over from the high-rises. There are thirty or forty of us now. Mostly men, some quite old. I recognize two of the *pétanque* players from the cement courtyard outside the Cinq Mille. I hear "*Mais allez-y*! *Entrez*!" from over by the cemetery, and see Karim standing on its squat rock wall, yelling for someone to go in. Other hoodie boys are gathering around him.

A static voice from a police loudspeaker responds, so sudden that I jump: "*Par ordre du préfet de la Seine-Saint-Denis: Dispersez-vous.*"—By order of the chief constable of La Seine-Saint-Denis, you must disperse.

I lean toward Free but still have to shout to be heard over the whirring. "They say we have to disperse, but I mean, should we? At what point does this huge press of people start hindering the police from going in?"

Free looks back at me, his eyes saying, *I don't know.*

Yaz has joined us and holds Khalil back from trying to jump the wall. The *grand frère* who had stayed behind with Sidi pushes his way through to us. He shouts to Yaz over the racket of the rest. "The ambulance arrived—they've taken *le jeune* to Hôpital Saint-Antoine."

"And?" Yaz shouts back.

The *grand* drops his eyes.

Sidi looked so bad. And the smell! Like a summertime barbecue, the grease that drips from the ribs onto the coals.

"Moussa!" I scream, and Free joins in. "Moose, Mobylette! Come out, it's okay!"

Now we all have to hold Khalil from rushing the wall.

From the rest of the crowd: "*Allez-y!*" and "*Entrez!*"

"*Par ordre du préfet,*" the loudspeaker booms, "*dispersez-vous.*"

Another police car pulls up, lights whirling, followed by a CRS van. They inch forward, pumping their sirens, but no one moves out of the way. We only clear a passage after two ambulances arrive, and then we open up an avenue.

An old man next to us, in a Muslim prayer cap, is close enough to the police to hear what they say. He says to another old man, "Did you hear that? The cop said that if the boys went in there, he wouldn't pay much for what's left of their hides."

The other old man says, "But why *if*? The cops know good and well the boys are in there. The cops are the ones who chased them in!"

The CRS people start piling out of their van. They wear helmets and carry big plastic shields, and it riles up the crowd even more. It riles me up too, because we're here checking on our friends, and the cops are just standing there, doing nothing but threatening us.

"Moose! Mobylette!" I scream.

"*Par ordre du préfet: dispersez-vous.*"

Some CRS guys spread out among the EDF guys; others take positions over by the cemetery, where Karim and the hoodie boys are. Karim doesn't back down. He screams and points his finger in the face of a helmeted CRS officer.

My phone starts pinging with texts from teammates. Free's too.

Where are you guys?

What's going on?

One from Adar: **Cops just let J-M and me go. 4 or 5 cop cars sped off. Are Moose/Sidi/Moby with you?**

I see Free turn off his phone, and I do too. What would I say?

That's when I spot him. Lieutenant Petit, the cop who stopped us outside the RER station after practice a few months ago, whose brother lives in Montreal. He's in civilian clothes, but even though he's out of uniform, I recognize his crab-apple cheeks and red hair. He's speaking with the old man in the prayer cap.

"*S'il vous plaît, Monsieur*," he says, "you have to understand, we're doing all we can right now." His voice is gentle, pleading almost.

"But the EDF," the old man says, "they just stand there!"

"They can't breach the facility yet," the lieutenant says.

"But why?" I jump in, like I have some clout because he and I have bantered before and I've got the upper hand, as if my being clever and white and from Montreal will spur him to action. "What are you waiting for?"

I can see he recognizes me too. He remains calm.

"Because it's totally unsafe," he explains. "There are twenty-thousand-volt transformers inside those walls. We can't do anything until the central service shuts the station down." He looks directly at me. "None of you is doing those boys any good crowding around, threatening the technicians."

And as if on cue, the loud whirring slows, like jet engines turning off. The transformers power down.

The crowd stills too. Shifts. The loudspeaker continues—"*Dispersez-vous*"—but the rest is silence. The dark night enrobes the high-rises, their windows lit up. Paris proper, someplace in the unseeable distance.

The old man next to us voices what we're all feeling. "There," he says to Lieutenant Petit. "Now go."

FREE

The technicians go in first. They wear tool belts and carry these big wrench-like things, and they have walkie-talkies. Summer-afternoon heat throbs off the compound, and one of the technicians takes off his jacket. The cop we know from before, Petit, goes to his car, gets behind the wheel and shuts the door. He just sits there.

It's not long before he raises his walkie-talkie to his mouth and speaks into it. We all see him do this, and the crowd shifts again. He gets out of the car and goes to the first ambulance, but not pressed, not in a hurry, more like he's lost in thought. The EMTs rush two gurneys into the compound entrance, and I'm thinking the dumbest thing I've ever thought. Seeing them gurneys, I'm thinking, What's going to happen with the game? Only four days left. If Moose is hurt, how will we replace him?

There's a collective gasp, then one huge sigh when a few minutes later the EMTs roll the first gurney out. On it, a body bag, zipped closed, bottom to top.

Right behind is the second gurney: another body bag.

The EMTs wheel the gurneys to the ambulances and slide them into the back. They close the ambulance doors—a loud *clack!*—and get in front.

The whole night pulses with light, like a disco ball on a dance floor, but all the dancers are still. Matt's face throbs blue then dark, blue then dark. Yaz, Khalil, stone still. I look back at Karim, the hoodie boys. Even the loudspeaker is silent.

The old man next to us moves first. He removes his prayer cap, his head collapsing forward onto his chest, his wrinkled hands wrenching and twisting the knit cloth.

A *grand frère* holds Khalil. Yaz says, as if to no one, "I have to tell Monsieur Oussekine." He turns, his face dazed, arms limp at his sides, working his way through all these people. I follow Matt, who follows him.

None of us says anything on the walk to the Cinq Mille. Behind us, we can still hear the police loudspeaker. "*Dispersez-vous.*" I look back, and even more cops have arrived, all blue-lit, but none of the crowd is leaving.

No one is doing anything. Most folks just stand there, looking at the substation or at the cops or at the CRS guys behind their plastic shields.

In the foyer of Moose's building, Yaz heads toward the stairs. Me and Matt follow. One flight. Two. Three. The dank smell of piss. French hip-hop filtering from somewhere down a hallway. When we get to their floor, the apartment door is open, Monsieur Oussekine in his *djellaba* already standing there. There's puzzlement in his expression.

We all stop.

Over his shoulder, I can see the little girl who greeted us and the other little ones, crowding the window, trying to make out whatever can be made out below.

Yaz steps forward. "Papa Oussekine," he says.

Then it shifts, Monsieur Oussekine's face. Not the rest of him, just his face.

"My son!" he cries—it fills the whole hallway—and he collapses against the door.

Yaz catches him and carries him inside. "My son! My son!" And the kids behind, stunned to stillness, look blank-faced at their father as the door slowly swings closed.

Me and Matt stand there in the darkened hallway.

There's a wailing from inside. Madame Oussekine.

We just stand there, me and Matt, the sound of commotion and "My son!" coming through the closed door.

Matt turns toward the stairwell, and we go.

He stops two floors below, heads toward an apartment and knocks.

"Sidi's place?" I ask.

He doesn't respond, just knocks more urgently.

There's no answer.

"They've got to be at the hospital," I say.

"Do I go there? Or call?"

Bad idea. He and Aïda have been hanging some, and I know he's worried about her, but Sidi's people need to be alone together. I say it as gently as I know how.

"Naw, Matt. Not yet."

He doesn't agree or disagree.

We leave the building.

"Should we go by practice?" he says. "Let everyone know?"

"There's no practice. They know."

We head toward the RER. Are silent on the train.

Matt says toward the window, "With the cops earlier, I was embarrassed. To be standing there like that, handcuffed. You know?" He looks my way, then back. "Like, ashamed."

"Wasn't nothing else to do."

"There's always something you can do."

"What?" I say. "What were we going to do? Bust the lot of them free?"

"I don't know." He looks me in my eye. "Maybe if we'd have run too, the cops would have come after us and not them."

Maybe. And maybe it'd be us zipped up in them bags.

I turn my phone on, and the list of text and voice-mail messages fills my screen. Two texts are from Françoise. The first reads: **Please call. Let us know you are safe. F.** I don't read the second. **Am fine**, I write in French shorthand. **Am not in Vllnve. Dont worry.**

At Gare du Nord, my transfer, I stay on the train. I mean, I don't want to have to explain this stuff, any of it, to Georges and Françoise. Or to anyone else, for that matter. I just want to hang with Matt, who saw exactly what I did.

Matt doesn't question my staying. We ride to Cité Universitaire.

FREE

I'm hoping Juliette won't be at Matt's place, but she is, and she's a hot mess. She comes running at Matt as we walk in the door, looking like she's been crying, and she scolds, "I called and texted! Why didn't you call me back?"

Matt lets himself be hugged. After she lets him go, she hugs me.

Matt plops down on the couch, and I slide down the wall and sit on the floor.

"You'll be more comfortable here." Juliette brings in a chair from the kitchen. "Or sit on the sofa beside Mathieu."

"I'm fine," I say.

She sits next to Matt. "When I didn't hear back, I almost called your parents." She pauses, like for effect. "*Putain*, kiddo. Your mother would kill me."

She lights a cigarette from a pack on the coffee table. Matt takes one too. Juliette doesn't say anything, just hands him the lighter. She drags on the cigarette a long time and then starts in again.

"So what happened? Did you know those boys that attacked the police?"

"Attacked the police?" Matt says. "Nobody attacked the police."

"It's all over the news," she says. "The radio and TV."

"Nobody attacked the cops, Juliette." Matt looks like he's about to cry. "We were playing soccer before practice and..."

"You were with them?"

"Freeman and me both. A bunch of others. We were just...playing soccer. And they chased Moose and Mobylette and Sidi."

"You were with those boys that vandalized and stole!"

"Nobody vandalized; nobody stole."

"The police chief says so. On the TV, on the radio."

"They're lying, Jules," he says. "I was *there*."

Matt looks dazed, at a complete loss. I don't know what I look like, and I don't know what to say either.

Juliette gets up and paces between the kitchen and the window. She crosses her arms over her chest, the cig dangling from her lips, her mind clearly working.

"They're spinning the story," she says, "to cover for the cops? You guys have to stay away from Villeneuve for a while then. Who knows what might happen now."

Matt is red-faced angry. "Don't you get it, Jules? It was Moose."

"I do, Mathieu, I get it."

"Moose!" he screams.

She goes to Matt and pulls him into her arms. "I get it," she says.

They sit like that for a while.

Finally she says, "So you have to do something then. Don't let them make your friends out to be criminals."

Matt and me spend the next several hours calling and texting folks while Juliette follows the media circus on the TV in her room and hollers updates to us. We call Coach Thierry, Le Barbu. I get Yaz's number from our DB coach, Celestin, but Yaz's phone just rings and rings. Matt talks to Monsieur Lebrun for a long time.

Juliette pokes her head out. "How about some sort of public protest," she says, "to counter all the spin?"

"We're on it," I tell her.

Matt jumps in. "There's going to be a silent march tomorrow from the electric substation to city hall."

"Good," she says. "The team's putting it together?"

"Some *cité* elders," says Matt.

"Even better!"

"Everybody knows," Matt says. "Everybody is outraged. They want to fill the streets to let all of France know the truth of what happened."

I look over at the clock—it's 3:00 AM. I'm exhausted. For real.

"Any news about Sidi?" I ask Matt. "Anything from Aïda?"

He shakes his head no and stares through the window into the dark outside.

I need to sleep. "I'm going to head home."

I had talked to Françoise earlier, told her I was okay and that I was at Matt's. When she asked about Villeneuve, I told her I was calling folks up there—which I was—but not a lot more.

Juliette kisses my cheek, and Matt walks me to the stairwell.

"I'll call you in the morning," he tells me. "We'll head up early."

MATT

First thing I do when I wake up is flip open my phone. Twenty-two new messages.

Juliette and I kept talking after Free left, and she's still asleep, curled up on the other end of the couch. I silence the ringer so the alerts don't wake her. Most of the texts are from Villeneuve, the same one forwarded from different people, confirming the silent march this afternoon. The message reads that kids plan on skipping school, parents on leaving work, for Moose and Mobylette and Sidi. But there's nothing from Aïda. I want news about Sidi, but I want to know how she's doing too.

A text comes in from Free: **Gare du Nord station in 45?**

I tap back: **30.**

I get there first and buy some Mars bars and potato chips at the newsstand on the far end of the platform.

"Check it out," I hear Free say.

He has *Le Monde*, holding it out toward me as he walks up.

"Looks like it got hot last night," he says, indicating the page the paper is open to. "They set some cars on fire, busted some windows out of a school."

"Did you see the interior minister's press conference?"

"I heard it. Why would he lie like that?"

"I wonder who's going to chime in next. The president of the Republic?"

We shake hands finally, a proper greeting. Then Free looks down the tunnel for some sign of the train.

"There's hardly nothing in the paper on Sidi," he says. "Just that he's in critical condition."

"And you believe them? *Le Monde* can't even get Moose's and Mobylette's ages right. Sidi could be dead for all we know."

An incoming text alert on my phone. It's my dad.

What happened to Moose?!?! YOU OK? Please answer my calls.

I don't know how he knows. The story isn't even twenty-four hours old, and *Le Monde* didn't mention Moose by name.

Juliette?

Then a text from her: **Your parents keep calling. PLEASE answer your phone.**

I didn't even feel it vibrate, but there is a list of voice mails. One is from my mom. "Please tell me you're not involved in any of this," her voice scolds.

Still nothing from Aïda.

I turn my cell off.

The train is crowded, but at Villeneuve station it's even more packed, both platforms filled with people, North African and African and white, filing out the exits—old people in traditional robes, kids like us in jeans and T-shirts, city workers in green jumpsuits. I wonder if they're Monsieur Oussekine's co-workers.

Outside the station *grands frères* from the Cinq Mille are giving away white T-shirts, *Morts pour Rien*—Dead for Nothing—printed in block letters across the chest. Police in riot gear—bulletproof vests, body armor, plastic shields—stand clustered in groups. Even more are in their white buses. They stare out over the crowd.

The Diables Rouges are set to rendezvous at the Beach. Free and I stand in line for our *Morts pour Rien* shirts, and then we head that way. *Le Monde* talked about "an urban disturbance," broken windows and torched cars, but everything looks pretty much the way it always does. On one corner, Free points out what's left of one of the city's plastic trash bins—a dark green circle, melted onto the sidewalk.

We head up Rue du 19 Mars 1962. At the end of the block are two unmarked cars full of cops. "It's funny," Free says. "They just sit there, like they're waiting."

"Must be scared of the march."

"With all these folks here?" says Free. "I'd be scared too."

There's already a big gathering when we arrive at the Beach. Many faces look familiar—friends and family of teammates. I see most of the guys that we were with when the cops charged us. Jean-Marc. Ibrahim. Off to the side, crying, is Adar. And the reality of it hits me again, suddenly, harder than any hit I've ever taken. Moose is gone. Mobylette too. Maybe Sidi.

I turn my phone back on. There are more messages, but I ignore them and punch out a quick text—**Please know I am thinking about you**—and send it to Aïda.

More and more people arrive. We're seventy or eighty now, milling around, greeting one another with handshakes but staying mostly silent.

It's nearly four when Monsieur Lebrun finally climbs the bleachers, Yaz behind him. Behind Yaz is an imam. He wears a dark turban and has a bushy beard.

Monsieur Lebrun speaks into a bullhorn, his voice crackling. "We're here to pay respect to fallen...Be respectful of..."

The imam follows. "The families are grieving...Our unity and silence must honor..."

I don't really hear much of it, or maybe it just doesn't stick.

Coach Thierry and one of the senior team players unfurl a twenty-foot banner that reads the same as the white T-shirts everybody is wearing: *MORTS POUR RIEN*. The rest of us crowd behind. We exit the Beach and slowly head toward the substation. It's not far, but it takes nearly twenty minutes to get there, the mass of us making the going slow.

A huge crowd is already there. The mayor of Villeneuve stands near the front. We wait in silence for a while; I look at the gray sky. Finally the mayor lays a wreath on the wall Moose and Mobylette and Sidi climbed over. He makes a short speech, offering condolences to the families, reminding us about the fragility of life.

"Like we don't know already," says Free.

"*Tchut!*" Coach Thierry snaps.

The mayor heads the procession, beside the giant banner. Our march is really a kind of side-to-side rocking, the size of the crowd so huge and the pace so slow. We number in the hundreds easy, hundreds and hundreds, pushing in the direction of the town center. Free and I are forty or fifty people back from the front, with our teammates.

We walk past six-floor walk-ups, rows of bunker-like bungalows. People stare from windows. A few hang sheets made into impromptu signs: *Morts pour Rien*. One reads: *Nos Fils!*—Our Sons. Some watchers join us.

On the Rue de Sévignié two busloads of cops wait for us. Two more arrive as we push onto the street. CRS in full gear line both sidewalks. Behind their helmets and visors, they remind me of Cylons, and because the street is so narrow, they seem right on top of us.

We ignore them and march on. The crowd gets pretty dense; people start spilling up onto the sidewalk. The cops use their shields to force them back into the road. Some shove with their telescope batons. They bark at us to stay in the street. The police have set up metal crowd-control barriers at the corner that force us to go left, toward the Charlotte Petit roundabout.

Jorge, next to me, grumbles, "Dirty pigs. This adds a good kilometer to our route, through Ville-Blanche."

Overhead, a police helicopter appears out of nowhere. It flies real low in circles above us, its engine roaring, its rotors whipping up waste paper and dirt. The dust gets in my eyes. I hear Coach Thierry shouting over the helicopter's rotors, something like "Remain calm..." and "...pay tribute to our teammates."

At the roundabout, a cop in full body armor starts to laugh for no apparent reason. I don't initially hear him, but I hear Jorge—"Our friends are dead, and you think it's funny!"—and when I look, I see the broad, mocking smile through the clear visor. The cop is giving Jorge a you-want-something-with-me look.

I hear Free tell Jorge, "Relax, *mec*."

Jorge is six-four and weighs at least two-sixty. "*C'est quoi ton problème*?" he snaps at the cop. "*Tu me cherches*?" What's your deal? You want something with me?

"Let it go," Free says. And I see Coach Thierry heading back toward us.

But it's too late. Jorge says, "Fucking murderers!" and he spits into the cop's visor. A plainclothes cop next to me, who I hadn't noticed, pulls out and flicks open a steel T-baton and strikes Jorge on the back of the head—*plink!* Just like that.

Jorge's head splits open, a bloody pink gash, and he collapses onto all fours.

It's like everyone around me is suddenly still.

Then it's all motion and commotion. "Dang!" I hear—Free—and then people are pushing, running in all directions. Screaming. A stampede.

I lean over Jorge, trying to protect him from the crowd. Free does too. Jorge is not out, but he's dazed, sitting in the middle of the street, his eyes glassy.

The next bit happens in slow motion. I see from the corner of my eye the riot cop who was grinning, rearing back to take a broad swing at us with his T-baton. I raise my forearm over my face—it's just instinct—but Freeman pops up and straight-arms him in the chest, which sends the cop flying back into the metal railing, his helmet askew, other cops dropping their batons to catch his falling body.

"Break!" Free screams, grabbing Jorge by the arm. "Go, go, go!"

Free and I are struggling to get Jorge to his feet. People jostle us. I hear whistles blowing—the cops. One sprays a canister into the air. I can feel my lungs fill with thickness, my eyes burning. But we have Jorge up, and we're moving.

With the crowd, which is moving away from the roundabout. Away from where the mayor is, at the head of the marchers—which is where, it seems to me, we should be heading. They wouldn't attack the mayor, would they?

I'm wiping at my eyes with one hand; Jorge's arm is in the other. We're trying to push out of this mess.

"Don't rub," Free shouts, his face scrunched and his eyes squinting. "The tears will clear the crap out."

It's hard to breathe. We're all three coughing, pushing toward a nearby alley. *L'Allée du Côteau*, the sign reads. Men and women and kids, running. Cops among us, swinging. Jorge kind of gets his wits back, and he's running on his own now, crimson wet all over his face and his white *Morts pour Rien* T-shirt.

At the top of the alley, on Rue des Près, a pack of CRS runs toward us, full steam. We take off in different directions—Jorge in one, Free in the other. Not because we're trying to split up; just because we do. I follow Free. We run along a row of closed-down warehouses and, at the top of the street, climb the cement stairs two by two.

We're in a kind of plaza, the top of city hall visible above the buildings on the other side. Hardly anybody else here. No cops. We lean over, catching our breath, both of us still coughing from the pepper spray.

Free says, "What just happened?"

"Dang," I say, my throat raw and burning.

"Dang is right," says Free. "For real."

MATT

Night is falling fast. The police helicopter flies circles above the plaza but ignores us. It points its searchlight at a cluster of hoodie boys that Free and I hadn't noticed, huddled beneath a tree at the other end. When the light hits them, they run.

"Look," Free says, pointing toward the Cinq Mille.

A chimney of orange-black smoke rises from between two of the buildings. Two fire trucks zoom past, sirens blaring, followed by a CRS bus. We dodge behind a tree.

"We got to get out of here," Free says. "The RER, bus, something."

"Cops were all over the RER earlier," I say. "And will it even be running?"

We both take a knee beneath the tree.

"City hall?" I suggest.

"Cops will definitely be all over there."

"But it's where the march was supposed to end up. And the mayor will be there."

He doesn't look convinced. Still, we start walking that way, fast but not running. Voices and odd noises fill the air. Spurts of laughter—one a high-pitched cackle. Glass breaking. Dogs barking, one baying. Down the street, Free and I see two cars side by side, burning. Four or five guys, hooded and with bandannas over their faces, dance around them. The windshield of one car explodes as we watch.

A police minivan arrives, and the hoodie boys dart away into an alley. The van slows to turn and follow them in. But it's an ambush! A larger group, maybe ten hoodie boys, encircles the van and starts hitting it with sticks and metal pipes. And I'm like, *Wow*.

The van shifts into reverse, peels out backward, but it hits one of the burning cars.

A cop fires a Flash-Ball from his window into the hoodie boys—*pop!*—and a boy carrying a metal pipe takes a direct hit; he comes straight off his feet.

Another shot. This time the Flash-Ball splits a green plastic trash bin in two.

"Jesus, Matt, wake up!"

Free is screaming at me, tugging at my sleeve.

"We gotta break!"

We sprint away from the ambush as other police vans arrive. We hear a siren coming from the direction we're moving in. Free cuts hard toward the Avenue des Quatre Routes—which leads away from city hall—but we're sprinting like crazy, no time to discuss it. We're just running.

The avenue is jammed with people going in every direction. There are thudding explosions and, before long, the smell of tear gas. A green municipal bus burns, orange heat and black smoke rising from it. People—passengers—stand huddled off to the side under the awning of a bakery, coughing, shielding their faces. A woman in a long coat lies on the ground. Two other passengers tend to her. She looks burned pretty bad.

A little farther on: a white tank-like thing, with a cannon in front. I only recognize what it is as the cannon fires full blast on us. The jet of water knocks me off my feet; it's like getting rammed by a tree trunk. Free collapses backward too.

CRS charge from behind the tank. I help Free up, but there's nowhere to run, nowhere without cops or water spraying or people falling over each other.

"This way!" I scream, indicating the alley between the bank and the pharmacy, but there are people everywhere and suddenly no Freeman.

"Free?"

People pushing, running.

"Free! Freeman! Free!"

Cops swinging.

I can't just stand here. I take the alley, Allée Victor Hugo, hoping this is the way he went, as it leads to the Cinq Mille. Somewhere familiar. That's where we'll find one another again.

But I end up face-to-face with a cop in full riot gear. Before I can dodge or duck or even flinch, he flips up the dark visor of his helmet.

"No," he tells me, "that way," pointing with his baton.

But it's like a disconnect. I can't make sense of his familiar face inside the dark helmet or fit the directions his mouth speaks at me with my immediate task, which is finding Free.

His hand is grasping my arm. "Listen to me, Quebec!" he says, and I recognize him finally: the cop with a brother in Montreal, Lieutenant Petit. "This isn't a game. There's a corps of CRS up there. Go that way instead. Now!"

And I do. I run toward the alley. It's long, all the doors and shutters closed. I run past a burning car. The heat singes my cheeks.

Right, onto Rue Berlioz. There's hardly anybody on the street, so I slow to a jog but keep moving. I try to call Free on his cell. Straight to voice mail.

Left, onto Rue Malraux. And there, just ahead, is about a dozen CRS, marching in the other direction. I stay far enough behind that they don't notice me. They turn the corner—and five hoodie boys with bandannas and scarves tied bandit-style over their mouths spring out from between two buildings! They pelt the cops with rocks, then run.

Toward me.

I'm running too.

The first of the hoodie boys catches up. We turn the corner together.

Helmeted CRS with dark visors masking their faces are there. They're firing guns. At us!

The hoodie boy ducks behind a car. Me too. Gunfire pop-pops off the side of the car, off the wall behind us.

"Rubber bullets," the hoodie boy says. "Don't sweat it."

Karim. I recognize his voice.

A helicopter whoosh-whooshes above, its searchlight looking for us.

Riot police beat their shields with T-batons and march to the cadence.

People at windows above throw pots and pans down at the police.

Karim pulls his cell from his pocket and flips it open, reads the screen. "C'mon!" he says and takes off. And I do too.

We're scaling a padlocked gate two buildings down. We cut through a deserted lot, climb a brick wall and jump into an alley. I have no idea where we are.

Karim's path leads to a parking lot. He stops and plops down on the ground, his back against the tire of one of the few cars remaining. I slide down beside him.

He pulls down the bandanna and reaches a hand toward me.

"Got a smoke?"

MATT

We're behind Moose's building. I recognize it now. Renoir.

We sneak a look over the hood of the car. It's chaos all around. Bus-stop shelters and phone booths vandalized and scorched. The entire area reeks of wet burnt chemicals.

The courtyard between buildings, forty, fifty yards away, brims with cops in tight groups. Clusters of guys, most with their faces covered, launch stones at them, then duck back behind park benches and trees. The cops pick up the stones and chuck them back. Stuff comes raining down from windows and from the roof—scrap metal, a toaster, books. A Molotov cocktail lands beside one knot of cops, the flames bursting in a spray of red over the ground. The cops scatter but regroup right away.

One boy gets too close. The cops swarm him, punching and kicking him. A police van comes screeching to a stop beside them, but the cops keep on. Kicking and kicking.

I pull a rock the size of a baseball out of the ground, screaming, "Fucking murderers!" as I launch it at the van. It sails through the air and hits; the windshield splinters.

The cops don't let up on the kid.

I'm searching for another rock. "Here," Karim says, and he hands me a bandanna. I tie it over my mouth and follow him.

We sprint from the car to a side street off the parking lot, what sounds like gunfire in the distance. The street is old, cobbled. Two more hoodie boys catch up to us, and Karim and the two others start prying a paving stone loose. I start in too, prying stones free. One hoodie boy takes off his sweatshirt and ties the top closed, and we use it as a sack. I feel searing pain in my fingers, and when I raise them to my face, they're covered in bloody gashes.

We get the sweatshirt sack half-full and Karim says, "C'mon." We follow him the long way around, to the other side of the building. Karim launches a stone at a line of cops standing thirty yards away. He reaches back. I hand him one and take another for myself. Mine fits in my hand like a miniature football. I throw a spiral, wobbly but true: it arcs, then hurtles down and into the visor of the helmet of a cop leaning out from behind a tree, hitting him flush in the face. He drops in a heap and does not move.

"*Ouais, mec*!" Karim says, and the other boys cheer me.

We have to fall back behind some trees, but when the rubber bullets stop pinging around us, I throw another stone. Then another. One of the hoodie boys screams, "*Liberté, égalité, fraternité*!" as he winds up and launches. I join in. With each volley, the four of us shout France's national motto. Under the bandanna, I can feel myself smiling.

Karim taps my shoulder. The sweatshirt sack is empty. We fall back but don't go to the cobblestone street. Karim leads us behind the building and into an underground car park. We're tossing knuckles and laughing.

"*Trop* cool!" one hoodie boy says.

"I got a text from Pierre," says the other. He pulls down his bandanna. "Molière High School is destroyed!"

"*Tchut!*" Karim warns, and we still.

There is a beating of feet on the concrete ramp. We all tighten—I'm ready to run.

Three hoodie boys round the corner.

"*Ouais, mecs!*" Karim says.

They all greet each other. Me too.

"Did you guys get some?" one of the new boys says.

"It was us that got the pig van on Rue Blériot."

"We heard about that!"

Another of the new boys says, "We did you better. Came upon a pig by himself."

"No!"

"Got him on the ground. Stomped him till his buddies showed up."

Another says, "I felt his ribs crack under my Timberlands."

"*Ouais!*" Karim says.

"It's just the beginning," the leader of the new boys says. "Villeneuve is hell for pigs tonight."

He removes a book bag he's wearing and sets it carefully on the ground as we circle around. Then he pulls his *Morts pour Rien* T-shirt over his head. The butt of a pistol sticks out of the waistband of his jeans. We all see it. No one says anything.

"Jacques texted," the leader says. He's taking glass Evian bottles filled with what smells like gasoline out of his book bag. He lines them up and begins tearing the T-shirt into strips. "He says the cops are regrouping at the Quatre Routes."

Karim helps him, pouring gas over the strips and stuffing them down into the mouths of the bottles. "At the Quatre Routes?" he says. "Let's go greet them."

The leader takes the sweatshirt we were storing stones in and puts it on, they load the bottles back into the bag, and we take off up the ramp. There are a few boys at the top, who join us. We jog down a dark alley, the streetlamps shot out. I let myself fall behind. And once we round the corner onto Rue des Près, I drop down behind a parked car. I squat there until I can't hear them anymore.

I'm breathing hard, panting. I rip the bandanna from my face, chuck it into the gutter.

"What the hell?"

I'm talking aloud to myself.

"What the hell was that?"

MATT

Behind me I hear police whistles. Up the road, an Esso gas station burns. Firemen spray water on the blaze, but they get bombarded from windows and rooftops and have to crawl for cover under their truck. I scoot away in the other direction, the direction of city hall. That's where I have to get.

But Freeman? Where's Freeman? Did I just do him like I did Moose and Mobylette and Sidi, leaving them when I should have done something, something that would have prevented what happened?

I stop and squat down beside a car. I try his cell again.

Straight to voice mail.

"Freeman, man. Come on, pick up. Let me know where you are."

Do I go after him?

But where?

Where I am is deserted and creepy quiet, but there are cops all around, and it's chaos out there. How can I find him with toasters and Molotov cocktails raining from windows, and cops everywhere?

I push on, onto another street, then stop and squat again. There's no one around. I walk on. I come to an intersection, stop again. Deserted in every direction. I pass the post office—a two-story gray block, every window splintered or busted out. The yellow-and-blue *La Poste* sign dangles above the main entrance by a thread of electrical cord. On the street in front are the scorched carcasses of three cars, one still smoldering.

Then I hear gunfire up ahead. An explosion—*boom!* Orange-black smoke streams up above the buildings. I hear police whistles headed my way.

Not again.

A couple rounds the corner, the woman tucked beneath the man's trench coat, his arm draped over her. They run toward me but duck into a doorway two doors up. I sprint there too before the door shuts.

It's a storefront mosque, and the guy at the door—he looks like a *grand frère*, though I don't recognize him—lets me in, then closes the door behind me. The place is dark but packed. Silhouettes, huddled together. There's murmuring.

In the corner, someone sobbing. I hear the ritual humming of prayer.

I stay near the door, by the plate-glass window—the only place where there's room still—beside two veiled women who *tchut-tchut, tchut-tchut* their whimpering children. I squat. Then stand. Then squat again, my face in my hands. I kind of want to cry. Or laugh. I want to feel something other than this.

The cop I tagged who dropped in the courtyard beside Moose's building didn't have a face. He was nobody, just a helmet and visor in a squad of helmets and visors. But real all the same. He could have been Lieutenant Petit. Maybe it *was* him. Just like maybe he was one of the cops who kicked and kicked and kicked that boy who got too close.

Real and not real. Like a music video, Rage Against the Machine, and all you can hear is a bass line thumping. Bandit-faced kids chucking stones and helmeted cops kicking and kicking. And him, the cop I tagged who dropped in a heap.

What have I done?

My phone's display glows fluorescent green in the dark of the room. *F-r-e-e-m-a-n* flashes as my ringtone, this silly jingle, starts up.

"Matt?" I hear across the dark, and I see a silhouette stand up.

I push my way to him. We meet halfway. Hug.

"You okay?" he asks just as I ask him the same thing.

Such a stupid question.

We look around, find a place to squat back by the door. Outside the plate-glass window, shadows sprint by, sometimes helmeted cops, other times hoodie boys. There are sirens, gunshots and, over everything, an eerie red glow: fires raging, just beyond where we can see.

We'll wait it out. We don't say so; we don't have to agree out loud. We both just know.

FREE

Normally, the first RER passes through at about five, so me and Matt cluster with a group of ten or twelve folks who've holed up at the mosque with us and intend to get out of there. Businesspeople, an imam, a bunch of women still carrying yesterday's shopping.

Outside it's still. There's broken glass everywhere and scorched cars here and there, and every now and then a group of riot cops that stare but leave us be. But by and large it's still. Matt is quiet the whole way to the station, just like he was all night—when I asked if he had been able to avoid the cops, when I asked if he had texted Juliette, when I asked if he had heard from Aïda.

On the train too. He's in his head, slumped down in his seat, staring out the window. At Gare du Nord I kind of hesitate. I'm not sure I shouldn't go on home with him to Juliette's. But I've still got Georges and Françoise to face. They wigged when I spoke to them yesterday, after Matt and me got split up and I ended up at the storefront mosque; they just kept calling and calling till finally I had to turn my phone off. Matt smiles at me, this fake smile. He says he's okay and waves for me to go on, and so I do. I go.

Françoise is on the couch in a robe, puffy-eyed, when I walk in the door, and Georges comes charging out of his office. "*Ah, mon dieu, mon dieu*," he says, his eyes all red and puffy too. They don't wig or holler or threaten to send me home right that instant. They start in to hugging on me so much I can't hardly move or breathe, and Georges keeps saying, "*Ah, mon dieu, mon dieu*."

I repeat the lie I told them from the mosque—that I was in Villeneuve when it popped off but found shelter right away and was never in danger—and when they finally quit peppering me with questions, I let on that I'm more sleepy than I actually am so I can get off to myself in my room. I close the door and strip off what I've been wearing twenty-four hours straight now, the *Morts pour Rien* T that still smells of newness but is sticky and stiff with soot and dried sweat. I rinse my face and my neck, my hands and arms, at the little sink in the corner.

I sit on my bed. I can hear Georges talking on the phone. "Yes, yes, he's all right," he says.

I try Matt's number to see if he got in okay. He doesn't pick up. Maybe I doze off, maybe I don't—it's hard to say. My mind keeps rewinding all the madness from yesterday so that it feels like I'm wide awake the whole time. But before I know it, it's going on noon. I turn onto my side, close my eyes, and then it's half past six.

I try Matt again. His phone rings and rings. I shoot him an email. There are all kinds of emails in my inbox from everybody, but nothing about Sidi. One from Marc Lebrun is calling a general assembly of the entire team for tomorrow, Saturday, at three at Villeneuve city hall, and I'm like, *Right. Go back up there? Who knows but that stuff might start popping off again?*

I try to write Mama an email but can't find the right words. Françoise knocks on my door to let me know dinner's ready. She still looks all happy, like I have risen from the dead.

Georges brings in the radio from the other room, and we listen while we eat. The news station reports that there were thirty-seven arrests last night, that twenty-eight cars got torched, along with that city bus me and Matt saw. They say twelve people had to be hospitalized, and I wonder if they're including Sidi.

A reporter breaks in, and, sure enough, there are "new outbreaks of violence in Villeneuve, in the Cité des Cinq Mille," he says, the sound of tiny explosions in the background.

We leave our plates and go into the other room, turn on the TV. Georges and Françoise see exactly what it was I went through. Cars burning. Riot cops and kids with bandannas over their faces, sparring. Chaos. The news cuts to a storefront, and I recognize it right away.

"That's where Matt and I hid out!" I tell them.

It's surrounded by police cars and CRS vans, the cops have fired tear gas canisters inside, and I'm like, "What's that about?" Folks—women in headscarves, with little kids, and old men in *djellabas* and skull caps, no hoodie boys among them—come spilling out, coughing and covering their mouths with their hands. The cops grab them up and push them, pretty roughly, into the back of a police van.

"But...what an aberration!" Georges says. "What could those elderly people have done to warrant such treatment?"

They both look to me, like I can explain it.

They stay glued to the set, but I go to my room. I try Matt's cell to see if he has the news on. I get his voice mail. I try again at nine thirty, at ten fifteen, at eleven, before nodding off. He never answers.

My phone wakes me—early, like six thirty. It's Juliette.

"Freeman." I can hear she's sobbing. "He won't speak to me. He just lies there. He won't even remove his bloody clothes."

"Bloody clothes?"

I hadn't even noticed. We were both all sooty and grimy.

"Still," she says. "Since yesterday."

"I'll be right there."

When I come out of my room, dressed to leave, Françoise, who was in the kitchen baking or some such, stands between me and the door. "You disappear during the troubles two nights ago, and now?" Her eyes are more pleading than angry. "Please, please, Freeman, don't return there anymore."

"I'm not," I tell her. "It's Matt."

She looks like she doesn't believe me. Georges comes out of their room in a bathrobe.

I take Françoise's hands in mine and turn to face Georges. "You have to believe me. I am not putting myself in danger. I'm not. It's Matt. He's having trouble."

I write Juliette's number down on a scrap of paper.

"Here is his cousin's telephone number. I will be there."

Françoise steps aside. She kisses me like Mama would, not the peck-peck-peck on the cheek like usual, but so as the kissing says, *I trust you; don't do anything that will let me down.*

FREE

Juliette opens the door but doesn't greet me. She just turns and leads me to her room, where Matt is lying curled up in a ball on top of the covers and facing the window. He's still got on the *Morts pour Rien* T—everything he was wearing the last time I saw him. Even his shoes.

I sit on the bed, down by his feet. "You okay?"

Such a stupid question, the answer obvious.

Juliette leans against the doorjamb, a cigarette in her hand that she ain't even smoking.

"Is it Sidi?" I ask Matt. "Did you hear something from Aïda?"

He doesn't say anything. Doesn't even move.

"Juliette," I say, as gently as I can, "do you mind?"

She backs out and closes the door.

"You got to let it go, Matt."

He just lies there in them sooty clothes, with finger streaks of blood I didn't notice the other day on the thighs of his jeans, across his chest, the nubs of his nails all scabbed over.

"Wasn't nothing you could do," I say, "about Moose and them."

He rolls onto his back, looks me in the eye.

"You don't know what I did," he says.

"What did you do, aside from survive when it wasn't sure any of us would?"

"I did more than that."

I see his face is streaked where he has been crying.

"You acted," I say. "You organized a march, and you got folks out into the streets. You helped Jorge when it looked like he was about to get stomped. You been looking after Aïda."

He turns toward the window.

"You don't ask to be leader," I say. "Something happens, and you act. It's just who you are."

I slap his shoe.

"Let's go," I tell him. "Get up."

» » » »

I stay out in the front room while Matt showers. Juliette sits in the window, dragging on cigarette after cigarette, her eyes dark, looking out over the rooftops. I figure him and me can walk a bit, over by Les Halles where he likes. He takes a long time, but I don't press him. The other day was rough. Rougher for him than for me, it seems.

Sitting in the storefront mosque all that time before Matt showed up and we found each other, I ended up thinking on things, just like Matt has been. On Moose and Mobylette, on Sidi. On Monsieur Oussekine collapsing, and Madame Oussekine's wail. What might I have done different so it hadn't all come to this? Or just what might I have done, period? Because it sure can feel like you did nothing when something like this happens.

But sometimes maybe we're all just flies on the ass of an elephant. The interior minister keeps saying that Moose and Mobylette and Sidi were juvenile delinquents and that we had been vandalizing the construction lot, so the police *had* to intervene. But folks in Villeneuve see straight through the bunk. The interior minister isn't just calling us vandals and thieves, Moose and Mobylette and Sidi and all of us that were with them that night. He's laying that charge on every kid from the projects. And kids keep taking to the streets, and what can you do about any of that?

Back home, after the chaplain and the casualty-notification officer showed up at our door and I decided to keep on playing anyway, I thought that was doing something. For my teammates, for my team. But I figured out quicker than quick that Pops wasn't any less dead for me doing it. Seeing Ahman and Jamaal and Juan watching me, seeing all my boys looking to me for...something—well, I just locked up. Now here I am, sitting in this apartment in Paris, my friends dead all the same, not for something I did or something I didn't do, but still, that's all I know to feel.

Responsible.

But that's not it, is it? Matt talks about how his pops always tells his teams about accountability. Maybe that's what we are, Matt and me: not responsible for what happened to Moose and Mobylette and Sidi, but accountable to them. Just like I'm accountable to my pops, to his memory.

Juliette, framed by the window, a cigarette in her lips, is staring at me. "You're going back up there," she says. "Aren't you?"

MATT

We leave Jules's building, Free and me, and the sun is blinding. Brilliant-blue sky and light reflecting off every windshield and every window. We head toward the RER station.

"You look like you're carrying a sack of cement over each shoulder," Free says.

I feel like it too.

I don't say this. I mean, what's to say? I'm finding it hard to be here in Paris. I'm not even sure what it was that made me want to come, all those months ago, or what it is that's made me stay. Some vague desire for freedom? To do any old thing—anything—regardless of what gets broken or who gets hurt? And I'm not sure why I agree to go to Villeneuve now. But I do. It feels like I have to.

Passing by the bakery, I catch a glimpse of myself in the window. There are dark rings under my eyes, and my skin is all saggy. Two cops stand on the sidewalk across the street, next to the pedestrian crosswalk. They wear regular duty uniforms and don't look mean or particularly dangerous.

Funny.

Free says, "Down here, it's like ain't nothing going on."

Down here, nothing is.

Up in Villeneuve, it's even stranger. The town feels as quiet as a country village. There are scorched places here and there on sidewalks and in the streets, but if I hadn't seen it with my own eyes, I'd think nothing had happened out of the ordinary. There's not a single blackened car carcass. The Esso gas station is roped off, but the post office is running like normal, people coming and going, all the windows replaced, the *La Poste* sign gone altogether.

"Feels fake, don't it?" Free says. "For show."

More CRS buses line the streets than usual, the cops inside behind tinted windows.

"But who are they trying to show what?" Free says. "Folks up here know what happens after dark."

We get to city hall and the general assembly is already under way in the main conference room. All the Under-20s look to be present, most of the flag-team players too. No Aïda. The mayor is seated at the front, beside Marc Lebrun and the coaches. Our fullback, Adar Traoré, swearing and waving his arms, tears into them.

"*Putain de merde*! The cops are everywhere and worse than before!"

Some faces light up when they notice Free and me standing just inside the door. Jorge smiles and lifts his cap and turns his head; there's a white bandage where he got struck. Free flashes a peace sign and moves off to the side, toward a couple of empty seats.

I don't know what I expected to feel, coming up here, but honestly I don't feel anything. Just blank. I follow Free, sit down beside him, as Adar starts in again.

"They beat my brother and his friend last night, sprayed tear gas in their faces and clubbed them! Just because they wouldn't submit to a random frisking."

"Yes, of course," Monsieur Lebrun says. "I hear you."

"And the mosque?" Salim Hassan, a backup linebacker, says. "Why shoot tear gas into a mosque during evening prayers?"

The mosque where Free and I hid out.

"Of course, I hear you," Monsieur Lebrun says, acting as a kind of proxy for the mayor, who just sits there, his head bowed. "The police maintain that it was an accident."

"An accident!"

"Come on!"

The mayor stands up then. "Perhaps it would be useful, and therapeutic even, if we held workshops for you as well as other youth, perhaps in the *cités* themselves, on how to properly express our anger..."

Jorge jumps out of his seat. "It's not our job to pacify the violence! We didn't cause it. The cops did!"

And a Cameroonian kid called Souffe yells, "It's on you, Monsieur le Maire! On the interior minister and the other so-called leaders who have allowed this to happen."

It goes on like that. Guy Martinez, who plays safety, says, "My papa's car got torched. Because...well, why?" And Claude tries to speak but starts to cry. He just slumps in his seat, the hulking mass of him, his shoulders lurching. Monsieur Lebrun is standing, asking us to be respectful and to please sit down, but it's everyone—Under-20s and flag players—screaming at the mayor, who is back in his seat, his face in his hands.

It's Freeman who regains control of the room. He climbs up onto his chair, so quietly I don't even see him do it. He stands there until all the others finally notice him too.

"Seriously?" he says. "This is the best we can do?"

The room is silent, all eyes on him. The mayor looks up at Free.

"We're gathered here screaming and angry, and we should be angry for what happened," he says. "But what are we *doing*?"

He looks over the room.

"Sidi," he says, "he's lying in a hospital bed, wrapped up like a mummy in bandages. Sidi, Moussa, Amadou—they worked so hard and would love nothing more than to play the Jets tomorrow. But they're not here, and so something would be missing for the rest of us."

I remember Free in Normandy, telling me what it was like trying to play after his dad was killed.

"Here's what we'll do," he says. "We'll boycott the final. We'll take the loss, we'll forfeit the game, in honor of our friends. Because they are more important than any game. But we'll do it actively, in suits and ties, like for a funeral. In front of the Jets and the entire crowd. So that everyone will know that Moussa and Amadou haven't died for nothing."

Everybody latches on to the idea right away. Guys begin tossing out suggestions: we'll make flyers with pictures of Moose and Sidi and Mobylette on them, spread them all over Paris; we'll create a web page and hit all the teams; one guy suggests we contact the Skyrock FM blog. Everyone agrees there's just enough time to get the word out.

My dad says you can read a person's true character by what you see of them on the field. I think back to the first Jets game, the way it ended—Free lighting up that kid at the final whistle, screaming at him—and realize that what my dad said isn't all true. What we do on the field isn't really a stand-in for who we are. Sometimes we do what we do on the field because there's a helmet covering up who we are as individuals, and we can only vent under cover of the group.

No, we are what we do when we're exposed, when everyone can see. And that person, if he has the courage to, can change and grow every day. The Freeman I know is the guy from Normandy; from Moose's apartment, with Monsieur Oussekine; from this morning at Jules's place; and from here, just now.

My friend, Freeman Omonwole Behanzin.

I look over at him. He has sat back down and is looking at his feet, and he doesn't look back at me.

THE UNDER-20s CHAMPIONSHIP

DIABLES ROUGES V. JETS

APRIL 19

FREE

Stade Jean-Bouin is a real stadium: manicured turf, electronic scoreboard. It seats something like twelve thousand. The sky is bluer than I've ever seen. No clouds, no wind. No cop cars in sight either, no CRS vans, even though the stadium is full to capacity. Folks pack the bleachers and stand ringed around the field, not for the game but for Moose, Mobylette and Sidi.

Georges lent both me and Matt suits that don't fit either of us particularly well. Georges was solemn as we tried on one jacket after another, so unlike him. It was Françoise who tried to lighten the mood, teasing us and telling us how good we looked and that our families would be proud of what we're doing.

Georges and Françoise are in the crowd somewhere. Matt says Juliette is too. The only game any of them have come to. The Jets line the opposite sideline. All their players wear dark suits and ties like we do.

The crowd stills when Monsieur Lebrun and the mayor of Villeneuve guides the families out of the dressing room. They stand alongside us Diables Rouges in utter silence, faces blank, everything around us just empty air between earth and sky. Monsieur Oussekine, in a dark suit and tie that doesn't seem right on him, silent and erect, his arm around Moose's mom. Pinned to his chest is Moose's grandfather's medal. Next to them are Moose's brothers and sisters. Then Mobylette's people, the Konates: dark complected and in traditional African clothes, so colorful compared to the dark suits the rest of us wear. His big brother Khalil. The Bourghibas stand next to them: a huge family, eight, nine kids, Aïda, in a dark dress and her red-and-white Diables Rouges headscarf. Sidi's absence is loud, as though he is dead too.

Seeing them like that—the Oussekines, Konates and Bourghibas, pieces missing from the middle of their family pictures—well, it's been building in me: I got to get back. Back home.

The Jets' club president crosses the field, carrying this huge wreath. He presents it to Monsieur Oussekine,

Monsieur Konate and Monsieur Bourghiba. He says something to Marc Lebrun and Coach Thierry, then speaks into a mic, his voice blasting the stillness that blankets the stadium. "We will not accept a forfeit," he says. "This game will end in a tie, nil–nil. We will share the league championship, for your young friends."

The stands boom in a really electric applause, and it goes on as the Jets players, in single file, cross the field and shake hands with us, one by one. Each passing Jet offers condolences. I nod and don't say anything. The running back I tagged during our first game approaches. I lower my eyes.

As the procession winds down, I look over and Matt has left the line. He's standing near the end zone with Monsieur Oussekine, Marc Lebrun and the mayor. I step up beside Matt, who is just listening.

"We'll do our best," the mayor says.

"That's not good enough," Monsieur Oussekine says. His voice is shaky. "My wife and I, my children—Moussa's brother and sisters—we have no more tears, so many have we wept since what happened to my son."

"I understand—" the mayor says, but Monsieur Oussekine cuts him off.

"I don't think you do. We have no more tears, but that doesn't mean we have forgotten him. Moussa's dream was to work with the youth of Villeneuve, to teach and give back in this way. I want…my family and I want you to do something—something!—in memory of our Moussa and to honor his wish. For him and his friends."

Aïda has walked up, and Matt puts his arm over her shoulders. Tears stream down his cheeks.

» » » »

Afterward, me and Matt sit on the Pont des Arts, the pedestrian bridge by the Louvre. Neither of us knows what to say. I don't, that's for sure. But I appreciate the sitting, the quiet and peace of it.

"Today," Matt says finally. "It's what my dad would have done."

"It was the right thing to do," I say.

Such a beautiful day. We just sit, our ties loosened, our backs to the railing, facing the Île Saint-Louis. Nobody seems to notice us.

I say, "I thought this place was a dream. Paris, I mean. Maybe it's really a nightmare."

Matt looks over at me, surprised. "No. There's always the good and the bad, the black and the white, both." He looks back out over the Seine. "You can't appreciate the sun without suffering the rain," he says. "My dad said that. Or maybe it was my mom."

I look out over the Seine too. Up at the spires of Notre-Dame, peeking over the rooftops. At the tiny patch of park below the Pont-Neuf, where there's a statue of King Henri IV on horseback, hidden behind a bunch of leafing trees.

The Pont-Neuf, I think, looking over at it. It means "New Bridge." Matt says it's the oldest one in Paris.

"You my boy, you know that, don't you?" I tell him. "For real. Always will be. Here, there, wherever. No matter what, I'll get your back like you've always gotten mine."

He doesn't say anything. The Seine flows on by below. Bateaux Mouches, all the tourists.

MATT

We sit at Nouvelles Frontières on the Boulevard Saint-Michel, the travel agency that the Diables Rouges used last January to change our tickets to open returns. The travel agents wear shapeless black skirts and loud red blazers. The one working with Free makes even that look good. She explains that the flights are full pretty much all the time now that it's after Easter, the start of the high travel season, and that his best option is one that leaves in two days.

"Two days from now is fast," I say.

"It is," says Free.

"You're going to miss my birthday. I'm eighteen in a week."

"I know," he says, "but I got to git."

I understand. I feel pretty sad all the same.

It's been three days since the memorial at Stade Jean-Bouin. There was no funeral for Mobylette, not here. The Konates had his body sent back to Mali. The Oussekines buried Moose in Villeneuve but in a private ceremony, just them, in an undisclosed location to keep the press away.

Aïda told us that the doctors say Sidi is recovering well, but in the TV news reports that show him in his hospital room, he looks bad. Bandages and raw patches of skin and his eyes just empty. Every time, he's staring into the camera and pleading for calm (Sidi, of all people), because things have gotten wild all over France. There are silent marches and sit-ins, but kids are also burning cars and attacking the police. All over. Towns big and small, north and south, east and west. One night it's Clichy-sous-Bois, the suburb next to Villeneuve. The next night La Courneuve joins in. Last night the news reported cars burning in the projects in Toulouse, Lyon, Strasbourg and Marseilles. Nine hundred, a thousand cars torched before sunrise. The interior minister has declared a state of emergency in the "troubled areas," but it just seems to fuel the anger.

The travel agent next to Free's turns to me. "Monsieur Dumas, I checked like you asked earlier. Your return ticket is valid for another eight months."

"Great, thanks," I say.

The one taking care of Free types in his seat preferences, and he asks, "What's up with that?"

"I need to stay a while," I tell him, "to do Moose's work."

"Moose's work?"

Monsieur Lebrun had suggested it after I told him I didn't want to leave.

"I'm going to lead a workshop the mayor is organizing in the *cités*. He put me in charge of it."

"For real?"

"Monsieur Lebrun asked me to keep working with the flag team and the juniors too, to get kids to bring their game to the field instead of the streets."

"Dang, son. That's dope!"

"Aïda and I have an appointment next week with the entire city council to talk about creating a fund in memory of Moose and Mobylette."

He echoes me: "Moose and Mobylette. As it should be."

Then he scrunches his brow.

"You and Aïda? Are you two serious then?"

"I don't know," I tell him. "She moves me."

The agent hands Free his ticket, and we head out onto the boulevard.

"I was wondering why your moms came to town so sudden-like," Free says. "This staying business—I'm guessing that didn't go over so well?"

"Dad, he's been great. He said he'd worry but that he was proud."

"And your moms?"

"Well," I say, "she still thinks it's an ongoing negotiation."

» » » »

Mom set the rendezvous at this restaurant called Les Fontaines, just up from the travel agency. She's already there when we arrive. She just got off a plane four hours ago but looks as though she's ready to begin a staff meeting. She wears a dark business suit and a Chanel scarf, her glasses perched on top of her head. But her face lights up when she sees me walk in.

"I don't mean no disrespect," Free whispers as we near the table, "but your moms is hot!"

"For Christ's sake," I whisper back, "she's, like, fifty or something."

I introduce Free. It's clear from Mom's face that she was expecting me to come alone, but I knew better. And she recovers quickly enough. They make small talk during the first course (paté for Mom and me, a frisée salad for Free). My mom starts in English, but Free insists on French. *Where are you from? How have you liked Paris? Will you visit Montreal?* That sort of thing.

Once the main courses arrive, he's out of the conversation altogether. "Our agreement was that you would sign up for summer classes at Orford," she says to me, "in exchange for missing the spring semester."

"We went over this on the phone, Mom." I've been rehearsing this speech in my head since yesterday, when I told her I planned on staying and she announced that she would be arriving this morning. "I love you, but I'm not you."

Free cuts his steak, looking down like he doesn't know us and just happens to be sitting at our table. I don't blame him.

I continue, "You and Dad gave Manon, Marc and me great lives. Really, I couldn't ask for more. But just because you and Manon and Marc went the corporate route doesn't mean I want to or should have to. I know you and Dad don't see eye to eye anymore, but I also know you respect him. I'm not saying I want to be a coach. I'm just saying that being a coach can be a noble pursuit too. Or a community activist or a teacher or a bus driver, for that matter."

"So now you want to drive a bus," she says.

"I'm just saying you have to trust that I'm doing what I think is right and best for me."

"What *you* think is best for you? How can you know? You're only a child."

"I'm eighteen. Legally an adult."

"Well," Free says, "eighteen in a week."

Neither Mom nor I think it's funny. He returns his attention to his steak.

Mom removes her glasses, folds and unfolds them, worrying the blue plastic frame like a rosary.

"You and I are not so different, Mathieu. The good in you is what I loved, what I still love, about your father. And believe it or not, there's also some of that in me too."

"Then trust it, Mom. Trust *me*," I tell her. "And if I screw up, if I make a mistake, trust that I'll figure a way out of it."

"Who am I to say, Madame Tremblay?" Free says. "What do I know? I'm even younger than Matt. But I would follow him anywhere." He rests his knife and fork beside his plate. "What more can you want from somebody than honesty and the profound belief that he will always be the best that he can?"

"I'm outnumbered," she says with a laugh. "I know, I know. And I do trust you, Mathieu." She wipes her eyes with the end of her scarf. "I didn't come here to fight. I came to see my son, whom I haven't seen in three months and, from all appearances, won't see again for several more."

"You'll see me, Mom. I'll come home when I can. And you can come visit, come to Villeneuve and see the work I'm doing."

She puts her glasses back on, sits up straight. "So," she says, clearing the tears from her voice, "what's her name?"

"Her name?"

"The girl behind all this."

"This isn't about a girl!"

"Right," she says. "Do I at least get to meet her?"

Free laughs. "She's great, Madame Tremblay. You'll love her."

FREE

Matt's moms gets a cab to her hotel after lunch. Me and Matt, we saunter down the crowded Boulevard Saint-Michel.

"So how long you plan on staying gone then?" I ask.

"You'll be the starting cornerback at Iowa State before I return home."

"Then you'll be back in Montreal before the end of the summer."

He says he's going to stay with Juliette until he can get it all sorted out and find a place on his own. He says he's built a lot of capital with Juliette since the madness in Villeneuve, that she all but tucks him in at night, but that he needs to be independent.

There are people everywhere all up and down the boulevard, both tourists and everyday folks. Lots of cops too, eyeing the kids hanging at the Saint-Michel fountain, the ones who look like they come from the suburbs. That's when I notice her.

"How did it go?" Aïda says, hugging and kissing Matt when we walk up. "*Salut*, Freeman," she says to me.

"Mom's good with it," Matt says. "Well, she's accepting my decision anyway."

We cross the Seine over onto the Île de la Cité and pass in front of Notre-Dame. We work our way through all the tourists milling around out front. Matt and Aïda hold hands.

"Free is leaving in two days," he tells her.

"Really?" she says. "So soon?"

"Yep," I say in English—curt-like, to set the tone, because I ain't studying no tearful goodbyes. "I got things got to be done."

We walk on with no real destination, and it's just as easy with Aïda here as it was with just Matt and me alone. I see what it is Matt sees in her. She's cool like that: the kind of girl you imagine as your girlfriend when you imagine yourself in a movie. And I'm thinking, Here we are in Paris, Matt's new home.

Home.

For four months, this has been my home too. Georges and Françoise's apartment. The cobbled streets, where me and Matt wandered, discovering new corners of the city.

The Cinq Mille projects. The Beach. In San Antonio, home was the house Pops bought and that him and Mama and me and Tookie and Tina lived in. Heritage Park Huskies football was a second home—my boys, Coach Calley. It was for me what the Diables Rouges were to Moose.

Am I even going to feel that in Iowa, at State? Should I expect to? Mama, Tookie and Tina look to be in New Orleans for a while, maybe from now on. It's kind of like there ain't a home really for me to go back to.

Well, there's Mama. And Tookie and Tina. In New Orleans, sure, but there for me still and all.

As much as what Matt's doing sounds tempting, I couldn't ever. I wouldn't, not again. Mama, Tookie and Tina, they are my home. I need to go on and get my degree so I can make our home better. That's how Pops would see it too.

"This quick departure," I tell Matt. "I really *am* sorry to miss your birthday."

"Well, maybe we should celebrate it early then," he says.

"Oh, sure. Why not?" says Aïda. "We can go to the Champs-Élysées, to your Pizza Pie Factory, play a game of foosball against your bouncer friends."

Matt laughs. "Yeah, yeah, yeah…"

He takes Aïda's hand. "At home with Mom and Dad, when there's anything worth celebrating, it's always with Champagne." He pronounces it in French—*shawm-PINE*. He pulls out his wallet and flashes the credit card his father gave him for emergencies. "And I still have this."

"You ain't eighteen yet," I remind him. The drinking age here.

"Pretty close. What with you leaving, my birthday upcoming—I bet if I show them my passport and your plane ticket, I can convince them to let me buy a bottle."

For real.

"I don't doubt it," I tell him. "I don't doubt it one bit."

AUTHORS' NOTE

On October 27, 2005, in the Parisian suburb of Clichy-sous-Bois, three boys were electrocuted after climbing into an Éléctricité de France substation, running away from the police. They had been guilty of nothing more than growing up in a poor, racially mixed and crime-ridden neighborhood, one feared and marginalized by the rest of French society.

Just minutes before, the boys had been playing a pick-up game of soccer on a pitch near their high-rise projects. It was the end of Ramadan—the ninth month of the Islamic calendar, a time of daytime fasting—and with the sunset, the group of boys, many of whom were Muslim, were walking home for supper. After passing a padlocked construction site, the boys found themselves suddenly surrounded by police cars. A neighbor had called in to report (mistakenly, it turns out) that the boys were vandalizing the property. The police, armed with Flash-Balls—guns that fire rubber bullets—rushed up on them, ordering them to stop and produce their ID documents.

Tensions had been running high in Paris's poor suburbs like Clichy-sous-Bois. Populated largely by immigrants, many from France's former colonies in North and sub-Saharan Africa, the townships had become a toxic combination of all the country's social ills: a decaying urban landscape, pockmarked with overpopulated and poorly maintained high-rise projects; widespread under- and unemployment; inferior education; juvenile delinquency; and crime. In a speech the week before, Nicolas Sarkozy, France's interior minister (who would be elected president a few years later), had made sweeping and disparaging statements about the projects, describing its hip-hop-identified young residents as "*racaille*." Commonly translated as "scum," the word can also mean "vermin." Sarkozy vowed to "*nettoyer la cité au Kärcher*"—to clean out the high-rise projects with a power hose, the language evoking the work done by an exterminator.

Relations between neighborhood residents and the police quickly deteriorated. Sarkozy assigned the CRS—the riot squads, which have a reputation for viciousness—to police these neighborhoods. Frequent and repeated checks of identity documents became commonplace. Residents perceived the CRS presence as being intended to intimidate, not to protect.

When the police cars sped up on the group of boys in Clichy-sous-Bois, three of them—Muhittin Altun, seventeen, Zyed Benna, seventeen, and Bouna Traoré, fifteen—panicked. Fearing the aggressive police as much as the eventual wrath of their parents for getting arrested, they ran. Muhittin, Zyed and Bouna sprinted past the graffiti-covered wall of a cemetery, the police chasing after them. Ignoring the skulls and crossbones, the Danger–High Voltage signs, the boys climbed the concrete wall of the electric substation in an attempt to hide.

The pursuing officers saw them enter the site. One commented, "If they enter the EDF compound, they're as good as dead." Still, despite recognizing the danger, the police left the scene without attempting to go to the aid of the boys—a violation of French law. They later reported not having pursued them at all.

Not long after, the entire neighborhood went suddenly dark. One of the boys must have misstepped. A blue charge—twenty thousand volts of current—engulfed the three youths. Zyed and Bouna died instantly. Muhittin, his clothes burned into his skin, managed to climb out and stagger back to his high-rise.

News of the deaths sparked violent riots, first in Clichy-sous-Bois and neighboring suburbs, then throughout the entire country. Over the course of the following month, dozens of public buildings were vandalized and burned, and thousands of cars were set ablaze. Five people died. Though three thousand rioters were arrested, no police officers were found guilty of any wrongdoing, not even those who saw the boys enter the substation and fled the scene.

Zyed, Bouna and Muhittin's tragic story inspired us to write *Away Running*. Though our novel is not those boys' story, their story has allowed us to explore the promise and the failures of multiculturalism and the accountability we all bear for one another.

Please visit www.awayrunning.com for more information and go to our Study Guide for Teachers for strategies and exercises that can help you incorporate the themes of our book into your lesson plans.

ACKNOWLEDGMENTS

Many thanks to Paul Rodeen of Rodeen Literary Management, an old friend who had the vision to imagine this as a work of fiction when we were struggling to write it as nonfiction, and to Sarah Harvey, our editor at Orca, whose sharp eye helped make the narrative work. Thanks also to our former teammates from the Flash de la Courneuve—notably François Leroy, Jacques Tillet, Fabrice Delcourt and François Rouat—and to Frédéric Martin, for giving us access to people who had been involved in the rioting as well as to police officers assigned to those neighborhoods.

The English Department at the University of Illinois provided generous support from the start, and residencies from the Blue Mountain Center, the MacDowell Colony, the Texas Institute of Letters and the Yaddo Foundation gave us the time to get the work done. Profound thanks.

Portions of chapters seven, eight and thirteen appeared previously in different form in the literary journal *Callaloo* (vol. 34 no. 4, November 2011), under the title "Going Places." The essay that inspired the novel also appeared in *Callaloo* (vol. 32 no. 1, February 2009), under the title "Away, Running: A Look at a Different Paris."

DAVID WRIGHT and **LUC BOUCHARD** met as teammates playing American football for the Flash of La Courneuve in suburban Paris. David, a writer and teacher of writing, has since returned to Champaign, Illinois, a home base from where he sets out abroad, most recently to Bahia, Brazil, and Benin, West Africa. Luc now lives in Montreal with his partner and his two daughters. Along with *Away Running*, last year he also finished *Bras de Fer*, on the infiltration of organized crime into Quebec's largest construction union. For more information about David, visit www.davidwrightbooks.com, and for Luc, visit www.bouchardluc.com.